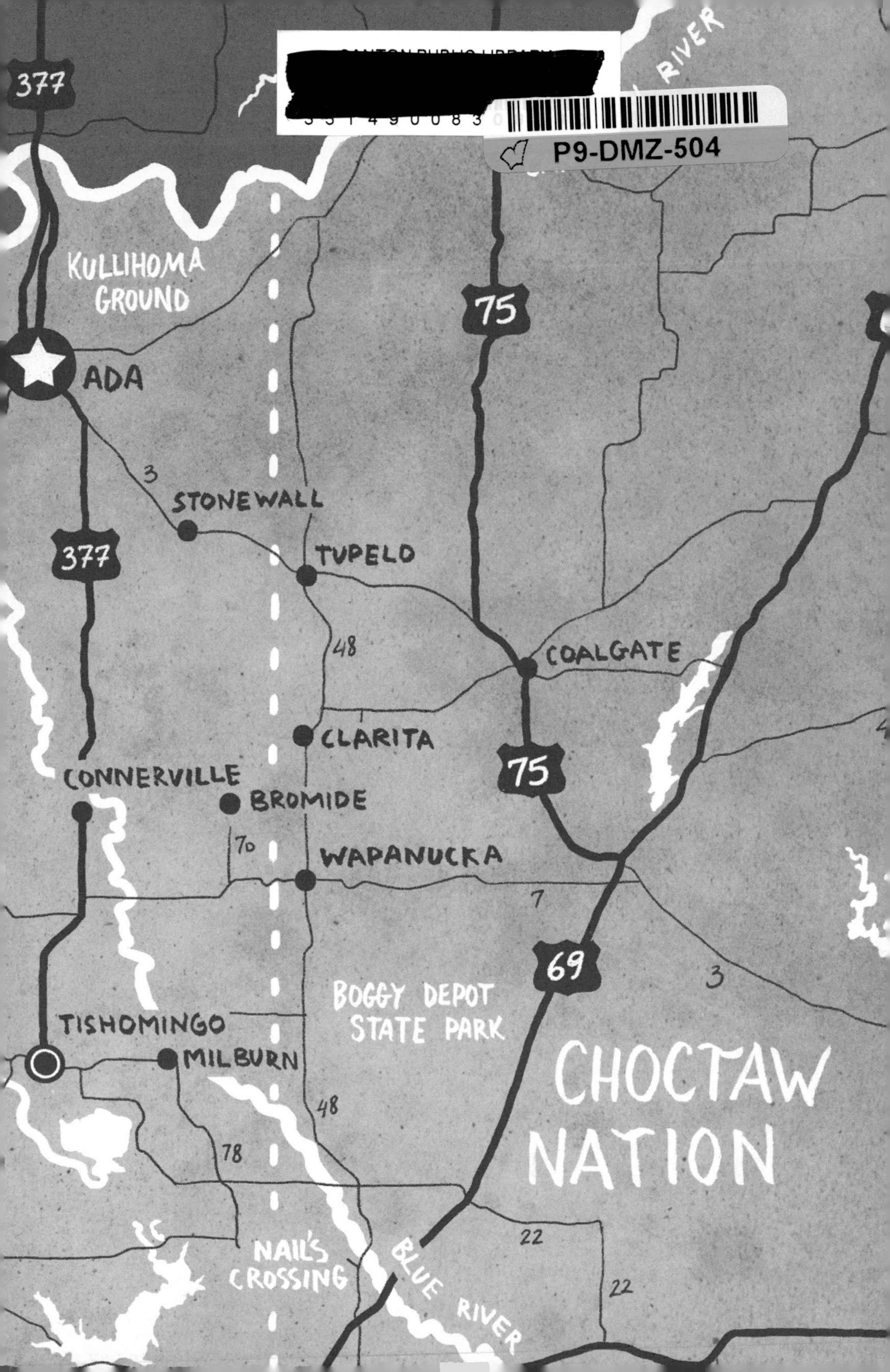
377
RIVER
KULLIHOMA
GROUND
75
ADA
3
STONEWALL
377
TUPELO
48
COALGATE
CLARITA
75
CONNERVILLE
BROMIDE
70
WAPANUCKA
7
69
3
BOGGY DEPOT
STATE PARK
TISHOMINGO
MILBURN
CHOCTAW
NATION
48
78
22
NAIL'S
CROSSING
BLUE RIVER
22

BUTCHER PEN ROAD

BUTCHER PEN ROAD

KRIS LACKEY

A NOVEL

Published in 2021 by Blackstone Publishing
Cover design by Sean M. Thomas
Book design by Djamika Smith

Printed in the United States of America

First edition: 2021
ISBN 978-1-9826-8927-8
Fiction / Mystery & Detective / Police Procedural

1 3 5 7 9 10 8 6 4 2

CIP data for this book is available
from the Library of Congress

Blackstone Publishing
31 Mistletoe Rd.
Ashland, OR 97520

www.BlackstonePublishing.com

To my wonderful sisters, Pam Camp and Amy Strohm.
To Sarah Miracle and Jill Fox,
who dedicate their lives to health equity
and Native American health.

CHAPTER 1

The boy stared at the ground as he walked out of a hackberry stand, toward Bill Maytubby's black Chickasaw Lighthorse Police cruiser. It was parked at a closed barbed-wire gap gate under a tall homemade ranch gate. Maytubby leaned against a fender and watched the boy approach. He had long black hair and wore an unzipped black hoodie over an old pearl-button Western shirt. The weathered ranch gate was made from two stripped-cedar king posts about fifteen feet tall, forks at the top supporting a crooked cedar crossbar. Not unusual in south-central Oklahoma. On one of the king posts, someone had long ago brushed "CHOKMA," a Chickasaw greeting, vertically in yellow paint.

Without looking at Maytubby, the boy came to the fence, pushed together the brace post and the gap gate post, lifted the top wire loop with his hand, tilted the gate post, and slid the bottom of the gate post up out of the bottom wire loop. While the boy was dragging the gate's limp strands and free posts to the side, Maytubby got in his cruiser, drove through the gate, and stopped. He lowered the cruiser's window. The boy was looking at him now.

"Thank you." Maytubby noticed that the boy was now watching his lips. "Three more police cars will be coming in a while." Maytubby held up three fingers.

The boy pointed down a faint vehicle trail, then opened his hand and flapped it toward the woods to indicate that Maytubby had a way to go. He dragged the gap gate back into place and secured its post with the wire loops. In the cruiser's mirror, Maytubby saw the boy standing still, watching the treetops for dust rising from the road.

The shallow wheel ruts wound half a mile through red cedar, hackberry, and blooming redbud before towering white sycamores loomed up from the banks of Pennington Creek. Standing motionless in the spidery shadows of their budding limbs, a woman of about forty, wearing a green cotton hoodie, watched Maytubby as he got out of the cruiser. He could see now that the sweatshirt said "Mill Creek Bullfrogs."

"*Chokma,*" he said, taking off his campaign hat.

"*Chokma,*" she said.

"I'm Bill Maytubby."

They stood quietly for a few seconds. In the distance, a quarry train blew for a crossing. Maytubby could see, fifty yards behind her, a small frame house with a tin roof and a brick chimney. A sun-bleached violet Dodge Neon was parked under a big pecan tree.

"He's over there," she said, turning her face toward the creek. She folded her arms across her chest and looked away from the creek.

"Thanks," Maytubby said. "I'm sorry, but there will be four more officers here within an hour."

She said nothing. He put his hat on and walked across a pebbly clearing to a rank of alder bushes on the creek shelf. He found an opening and edged sideways onto the rocky bank of a clear pool. A great blue heron regarded him from the opposite shallows.

The body was practically at his feet. It bumped against granite boulders that kept it from the little falls at the end of the pool. The torso, facedown on the gravel bottom, was clad in a sky-blue long-sleeved shirt and a two-tone gray fishing vest, both several sizes too big. A split-willow creel bobbed from a neck strap. The back of the vest was vertically scored with small rips. The legs, in cinched bootfoot chest waders, canted downward to a slightly deeper bottom. Also drifting in the eddy was a wood landing net inlaid with turquoise, tethered to the vest by a bungee loop.

Beside the boulders, a single metal wading staff glinted from a fallen cottonwood. An adobe-colored bucket hat lay half on the shore and half in the water, two dun fishing flies embedded in its wool patch. The fly rod sticking up from the water was bamboo. Thick mint-green fly line sine-waved toward the channel before dropping out of sight. Wet-tip line, for sinking flies.

Suddenly, the sine wave flatlined and the tip of the rod bent. Maytubby pulled out his phone and photographed the corpse and rod an instant before whatever fish had taken the fly pulled the whole rod and reel into the pool. The floating stretch of line looped and crossed like a skywriter.

He sent the photo to his chief, Les Fox, to Johnston County Sheriff Benny Magaw, and to Agent Dan Scrooby at the Oklahoma State Bureau of Investigation. The staties would be here shortly with their bazooka lenses.

Above the rush of the falls, Maytubby heard crunching footsteps an instant before a longer shadow than his own joined his.

"He's got one."

Maytubby nodded but didn't turn his head. "Hannah. Didn't hear your cruiser."

"That kid at the gate deaf?" She stared at the heron.

"Think so." The mint-hued line looped and crossed.

Hannah Bond extended her left arm toward the corpse and turned her palm up. "Since when does *Field and Stream* come to Bumfuck, Oklahoma?"

"I know. Important-fisherman suit."

"I bet his underpants have fish on 'em." She paused. "And if his underpants are as big as that outfit, how did he keep 'em up?"

The creel erupted with thrashing fish.

Hannah said, "Pretty sure that basket has a precious name."

"It's a creel."

Hannah wrinkled her nose. "Sounds like a ghoul."

The heron speared a fish, pivoted, and shook it onto the shore.

"Speakin' of," she said, "that's a nasty gash behind his temple."

Maytubby pointed to a large round rock a few yards upstream.

Hannah sighted along his arm. “Plenty of blood, but he’d have to fall anniegogglyn.”

“And from the top of this sycamore.” Maytubby looked up.

“Yeah.”

“Also”—Maytubby touched Hannah’s shoulder and pointed to the cottonwood snag—“he had a wading staff. The precious word for a walking stick. Has a metal point that sticks into the riverbed.”

Hannah squinted under her hat brim. “That thing’s metal except the grip. If it doesn’t float, how’d it get downstream in this piddly current? And tell me those things can climb. It hasn’t rained for weeks.”

“Closest public access to this creek is the national fish hatchery.”

“Four, five miles downstream,” Hannah said.

“I’ll tell the Medical Examiner’s Office to check for wader-boot blisters.”

“I’ve bait-fished and noodled. But this game”—she pointed down at the body, moved her hand up and down—“stumps me. I see dudes at it down on the Blue after the winter trout are stocked. Seems a little like strappin’ on chaps and spurs just to go feed the cows. Easier to stand on the bank with a Mr. Crappie and a can o’ corn.”

“And why would somebody even wade this little creek when it’s too early for snakes and ticks to be a big problem?” Maytubby glanced up and down the stream. “Brush, overhang, timber snags—and that rod must be nine feet. You couldn’t get even a decent roll cast in here. What’s the point?”

Bond now looked at Maytubby.

When she said nothing, he turned to her. “What?”

“Makes me wonder what else you got in your closet I never seen.”

He frowned and then raised his eyebrows. “Oh. Roll cast. When I was in college in Santa Fe, I had some rich friends from back east.”

“Mmm.” She nodded. “Trout year-round in the New Mexico mountains.”

“Yeah. But also stocked from the local hatcheries.”

“Don’t have to hitch a ride from Arkansas like ours.” Hannah pointed at the creel, which was now quiet. "I wonder what kind of fish are in that basket."

Maytubby pulled out his phone and touched its screen. "Called OSBI and the ME's office right after Dispatch got the call from Ms. Laber." He crooked his head toward the little house. "Owns the land. Originally an allotment."

"Passed into her family, still legally Indian country."

Maytubby nodded. "I'm going to walk around, try to get bars so I can call the office. Want me to call your boss?"

Hannah looked at her watch. "Twelve-ten on a Friday. Sheriff Magaw will be reciting the pledge with his fellow Tishomingo Lions. Also, you don't know where I'm at."

"Entangling me in your deceit, as usual."

"I delivered my summonses on the Big Rock. Perfessor."

"Point taken."

"I'll tell him after Lions. Try not to rub it in I'm here first."

Maytubby walked away from the stream, parting the alders. He held his cell phone aloft, circled his cruiser and the deputy's white Ford Crown Vic. The Vic had a lightning bolt through "SHERIFF." When he had two bars, he called Dispatch.

"Hey, Bill. You got a secret message that can't go over the police radio?"

"Hey, Sheila. Can't multitask on the radio."

"You know men can't do that, even on a phone."

"I just photographed a crime scene with this phone and sent the pic to Chief Fox and OSBI." Maytubby looked up at the little house. Deborah Laber stood in the front doorway, arms crossed.

"*Then* you called me. See, that's one at a time. I saw a report on man brains and woman brains on the *Today* show."

"So man brains can't multitask? That's a huge bummer, Sheila."

"Shut. Up. You're just too lazy to get in your police car. You find the body?"

"Yes. Just where Ms. Laber said it would be. Fly-fishing togs. Hat, vest, net, waders."

"On *that* little creek?" The police radio crackled behind her voice.

Maytubby opened the trunk of his cruiser. "I called OSBI and the medical examiner."

He grabbed a roll of crime scene tape and some yellow plastic evidence markers, shut the trunk. "You know, Sheila, while I'm talking to you, I'm getting crime scene tape out of my trunk."

"Not near the same. I'm never gonna hear the end of this. Should've let you live in ignorance."

"Bye, Sheila."

Maytubby slipped through the alders and stood beside Bond, who was stuffing blue disposable gloves into one of her duty belt holders. "Well?" he said.

"Rainbows," she said, snapping the holder.

He nodded. "Just an educated guess."

"You got it."

"Feds don't stock trout in this stream. Yesterday was the end of the season on the Blue. Hell of a lot of work for such a stupid plan." Maytubby turned to look at the woods downstream. "We can forget about wader blisters."

"Work and patience. They couldn't kill a trout fisherman in that last-day crowd on the Blue. Have to cruise the access roads, wait for one of the Dallas slickers to shuck his gear and go for a country leak. Gimme an end."

Maytubby held out the crime tape roll, his cupped hand through the spool.

Hannah said, "OSBI's not gonna like this." She took the loose end and walked into the alders. He followed her into the clearing where the cruisers were parked. Then she walked upstream while he waited beside a sycamore until she had tied her end to a tree at the head of the pool. He wrapped tape around a limb stump. When they had worked their way below the falls, Maytubby stopped and nodded at the ground.

"How far'd we drive off Bellwood Road?" Hannah said. "Half a mile?"

"Four-tenths."

"Stupid for sure, but some strong to drag that thing alone . . . Or maybe more like slow and patient."

"Hannah, you came from the east and then south?"

"Yeah."

"And I came from the west. You think if I went south on Bellwood, I might find the Texan's vehicle, too?"

"Last time that guy goes into the bushes to take a leak." Hannah massaged a taut length of tape between her fingers. "Except . . ."

"He would keep the keys in his pants," Maytubby said. "Or. Those other trout people have phones, too. We would've heard about a stolen vehicle."

"He could still've gone to take a leak. Thieved clothes—you'd want to keep that to yourself. Bet he stopped at Academy in Sherman and bought a new outfit so Dallas wife wouldn't catch on."

"Might have to drive a little farther for some of that gear," Maytubby said. "Like Maine."

"Or his office computer."

They walked sideways, parallel to the flattened path of the dragged corpse, keeping the path in front of them as they taped south and west away from the creek.

When the topsoil was deep enough to hold footprints, they slowed to study the ground, most of it covered in sycamore and oak leaves. A bird shadow shuttered the sun for an instant. They looked up to see the great blue stroking the mild air.

When they looked back down, a little breeze flipped some sycamore leaves, baring a patch of ochre ground. Both Bond and Maytubby pointed at a footprint. Maytubby quickly retrieved his phone, zoomed its camera, and sent the photo to Fox and the OSBI. He fished out an evidence pointer, swished away some leaves, laid the marker on a flat rock, and pinned it there with another rock. OSBI would later make casts of every print with dental plaster.

"Toe pointed away from the creek," Hannah said. "Would've been. Dragging *and* vamoosing."

"Shallow heel. Definitely vamoosing," Maytubby said. "Pronate."

"Smooth sole. And not a boot—cowboy or Wellie."

"Yeah. Dress shoe?" Maytubby said. He walked sideways, letting the tape unspool as Hannah followed, wrapping it around broken limbs. The gibberish of mockingbirds drifted from the overstory.

"Must be at least a thirteen," Hannah said. "So, likely taller than average. Man the size that fishin' costume back there would fit."

"How many times you think these blackjack limbs scraped the fisherman's hat off Bigfoot?"

Hannah snorted. "Can't you see that goober slappin' down escaped trout by moonlight?"

"How'd he keep them alive until then?"

"Sink 'em in the ice chest amongst his Keystones?"

* * *

Maytubby pushed through the alders and joined Bond between white vans from OSBI and the Medical Examiner's Office.

"Couple horse trailers, we could have a rodeo," Bond said.

"You recognize either one of those techs?" Maytubby crooked his head toward the creek, where he had left them to their work.

"I think the middle-school girl worked the Greasy Bend bridge murder last year."

"The ME guy must be in her homeroom."

The boy from the gate walked into the clearing, turned from the drive to join Deborah, who was walking from her house toward Maytubby and Bond. She put an arm around the boy as they walked together. "He's got her chin," Maytubby said. He removed his Smokey hat. When the OSBI tech returned to her car for something, Deborah Laber and the boy stopped and watched her until she had closed the trunk and disappeared through the alders.

"Am I okay here?" Bond said softly.

"Sure," Maytubby said. "She'll look at your nameplate and think you're one of the Chickasaw Bonds."

"There's a few." Bond looked away from their approaching company. "Anyway, more'n Irish Maytubbys."

When they arrived, Maytubby watched the boy watching his lips. Deborah Laber and Maytubby did not immediately make eye contact. Maytubby said, "Ms. Deborah Laber, this is my friend, Deputy Hannah Bond."

They half-nodded, half-smiled.

Laber looked at Maytubby. The boy looked at Laber. "Everyone calls me Deb," she said. He nodded. She turned her head toward the boy. "This is my son, Jason."

Jason's hands stirred as he moved his eyes to Maytubby. "Hello, Jason," Maytubby said.

"He's on spring break from OSD," Deborah said.

"Last fall, one of your Indians scored seventeen touchdowns in one game." Maytubby signed "Seventeen," turned his palms up. All he knew.

Jason nodded, then looked down. His mother touched his shoulder to get his attention. She said, "Dylan," while signing the name to him. He looked from her to the creek behind Maytubby, ran his palms up and down his jeans.

"They could only play six-man 'stead of eight that night." Deborah said.

"Flu?" Maytubby said.

"Pinkeye." Her voice trailed off as she looked toward the river.

Maytubby waited a few seconds for the murmur of the falls to ease his segue.

He spoke to Deborah Laber. "I see you don't have a dog. Were there any unusual noises last night?"

She made a moue and shook her head. "Before I went to sleep around ten, just the usual. Coyotes, train in Mill Creek, owl. After that, I don't hear anything until the alarm at five-thirty. My shift at Sipokni"—she pointed southeast—"starts at seven. I sleep like a log."

"Sipokni West—Old West. That's in Reagan, on the Big Rock," Maytubby said. "Never eaten there."

"Good fries and chicken-fried steak," Hannah said to Maytubby. Then she looked slyly toward Deborah Laber. "Sergeant Maytubby perfers rabbit food."

Jason looked at Hannah's lips with some confusion.

"Deb, did you discover the body? Or Jason."

"Oh, this fella did. He roams the woods. I was finishing my coffee."

"Jason mention anything unusual about the night before?"

The boy looked away from Maytubby's face and rubbed his palms on his jeans. "No," she said. Then she faced her son and signed as she spoke aloud. "You outside last night? See anybody around here?"

Jason shook his head hard several times, thrust out his right arm and signed "no"—index and middle fingers snapping against thumb—only once. Like a rattlesnake strike.

His mother frowned at his hand for a beat before she turned back to Maytubby—giving her face an extra quarter turn so Jason couldn't see it. "*That's* a weird no," she whispered, as if her son might hear.

"Right," Maytubby said. He reached to shake Jason's hand. The boy obliged. "Thank you, Jason." Maytubby took a business card from his shirt pocket and handed it to Deb Laber. "Use my cell number if you learn anything. The other investigators may be asking you questions after Deputy Bond and I leave. If you would, tell Jason we're both old hands with a gap gate. We'll let ourselves out." She was signing as Maytubby and Bond walked to their cruisers.

"You think we should split up at Bellwood Road to look for the decoy vehicle, or both go south?" Maytubby said.

"I thought you were worried about keeping me from my duty." Bond opened her cruiser's door.

"The spirit is willing. But let's both go south."

CHAPTER 2

The car was parked on the north side of a one-lane pony truss bridge over a dry wash, passenger-side wheels on a grass shoulder. Possumhaw bushes grew in the wash. Maytubby and Bond stood on the shoulder in front of the car. It was a rust-gnawed 1956 Hudson Hornet sedan with a bird's nest sprouting from the V in its grille. Its front Texas plate, tied to the bumper with baling wire, was current and shiny but dented in the center, top and bottom.

"You're shittin' me," Bond said.

"Gotta admire it, though. Kills the last detail—Texas bird's nest." Maytubby tied a little strand of crime scene tape on the passenger-side mirror.

"And there's the clown shoes." Bond pointed. Maytubby photographed the prints in front of the car close up with his phone, then snapped on blue disposable gloves and walked to the grille, avoiding the footprints. He forced a screechy latch and lifted the hood.

Bond leaned forward and peered in. "No battery, no belts." She straightened up and looked down the road. "Must be all downhill from Texas."

He pointed down to the license and bumper. "Bent his plate with the tow chain." He looked up at her. "The rope they used to tie the steering wheel still lying on the driver's seat?"

Bond leaned sideways, looked in the passenger window. "You called it."

Maytubby rejoined Bond on the shoulder. "How'd they find four tires? Even bald ones."

A dually Ford 350 pulling a horse trailer spun up a plume of yellow dust as it approached. The driver, wearing a straw Western hat, did not slow down but rubbernecked at the antique car. The dust washed over Maytubby and Bond. They licked it off their teeth and spat.

"That deaf kid was nervous," Bond said.

"I noticed that."

"Maybe just shy. What the hell are those?" Bond pointed at two sets of parallel tire prints, very narrow, about four feet apart. They appeared between the two tire tracks of what must have been the towing vehicle, which were also bald and curved toward the shoulder. "Clown walked between 'em, both ways."

Maytubby zoomed in and took several photos. "OSBI can measure. No tread on the narrow ones, either."

They looked toward the barbed-wire fence from where the narrow prints left—and returned to—the road. "Gap gate," Bond said.

"Snug," Maytubby said. "I didn't see it."

"Bozo did." Bond rested the heels of her hands on her duty belt. "Some brush, and not a house for a mile any direction."

"He just knows his Dallas angler. Who always parks far from the water and steals up on his prey through impenetrable undergrowth. 'Stealth' is his watchword."

Bond hawked a dust loogie and spat. "Everything with two wheels that far apart, they got a tread."

"Maybe it's a travois," Maytubby said.

"A *what*?"

"Sled made out of two joined poles, usually pulled by a horse. Sling between the poles to hold stuff. Plains Indians used 'em."

Bond looked at the tracks again. "I know that tech's just a middle-school girl, but you're gonna need her help."

CHAPTER 3

Maytubby's phone vibrated. "Don't tell me, Sheila." He spelled out the Texas plate number.

"Guy in Highland Park said he was so mad about his fishin' gear, he didn't even notice the tags were missing until now. Looks like you found 'em."

"On Spring Creek Road at Honey Wash. On a Hudson Hornet." He looked at Hannah, who studied the ground.

"Eisenhower times. One more Okie hillbilly tale for the North Dallas barflies." There were voices in the background. "Hold on, Bill." Her office phone clattered. He could hear her talking with someone on the police radio. The phone clattered again. "It's Jake Renaldo. He's pursuing a white ninety-eight Ram, just turned east off State One onto Sutton Lane."

Maytubby held his phone away from his face. "Hannah, Jake Renaldo's after a white ninety-eight Dodge Ram on Sutton Road." They jogged along the shoulder toward their cruisers. "Eastbound."

"Well, I hope," she said. Then she pinched her shoulder mike and reported the pursuit.

Maytubby brought the phone up. "On it, Sheila. Tell the OSBI agent about the Hudson."

"Right," she said.

He got in the cruiser, turned on the overheads, and led Hannah in a U-turn north. One-lane Sutton T-boned Bellwood about a mile north of them. Dust stirred up by the chase sifted into banks of red cedar. Maytubby slewed around two doglegs and then kicked the Charger over the straightaway leading to Sutton.

As he neared the intersection, the Ram topped a little rise to his west. Renaldo's Highway Patrol cruiser trailed it, curtained by dust. Maytubby turned left and stopped. Bond stopped behind him. He could see a long, slender arm sticking out of the Ram's driver's window. As the pickup approached, he saw that its hand held a cigarette.

He did not get a good look at the woman driving the pickup before it veered off the road, thumped through the bar ditch, and hammered a rock-pile corner post. After a comic beat, its hood sprang open.

Renaldo parked facing Maytubby and Bond. All three got out and walked slowly down and then up the shallow ditch banks. Steam rose from the pickup's radiator, coolant drizzling the stones. The officers stopped. A peal of hoarse laughter rang from the cab. With her inside hand, the driver pushed against the dash, got her torso back over the steering wheel and into the seat. She was middle-aged, her hair streaks of auburn and gray. Blood seeped from her scalp where she had struck the windshield. She held up the outside hand and looked at it.

"Shi-i-it," she cackled. She pointed vaguely toward Renaldo. "Cowboy there made me lose my cig'rette." She opened the door and swung her legs out of the cab, clinking two empty pints onto the ground. She held the armrest as she rose. There were burn holes in her sweatshirt.

She turned to regard the damage, then feigned a double take. "My brand-new white *truck*. Now it's a hog's breakfast." She pointed at it, turned, and glared at Renaldo. "You utterly ruint it." Her red eyes did not stay on him long but moved to Maytubby and Bond.

Her rage quickly gave way to mock astonishment. "Whadda we got *here*? Lone Ranger, Tonto, and the fifty-foot woman." She shook her head and grinned to herself.

"You want me to call Johnston County EMS?" Hannah pointed to her own forehead.

"And who'll be drivin' *that*?" the driver brayed. "Goat Man?" She wiped her head and looked at her hand. Then she wiped her hand on her jeans. "No. I ain't hurt. I am drunk. And how do you figure I'd pay Goat Man? My supposedly husband spent all our money on that city slut he sees in Tishomingo." She put her fists on her hips and smiled again.

Maytubby watched her face and squinted.

The laugh gurgled up. She wagged her finger at the officers. "But I fixed his wagon. For. Good." The extended arm threw her off balance, and she fell forward. Bond helped her to her feet and then held her left biceps.

Renaldo said, "Ma'am I need to see your license and registration."

With her free arm, she patted her jeans pockets deliberately, then pulled out a flattened pack of cigarettes and a red disposable lighter, both of which she held in one hand. When she shook the pack, most of the cigarettes tumbled onto the grass.

"Shit." She held the pack to her face, lipped out a survivor. When she turned her wrist to click the lighter, the rest of the cigarettes fell out. She took a deep drag and said, "Shit!"

A Johnston County sheriff's cruiser with its overheads flashing roared up Bellwood and braked hard. Dust swirled around the deputy as he got out.

"Katz," Renaldo said, half-rolling his eyes.

"We know what *he's* gonna have to say," Hannah muttered.

"Phoo-*ooo*," Maytubby whispered.

Katz waved dust out of his face as he walked along the shoulder.

The woman took a short drag and tilted her head. "Got-*damn*. I guess we can start lookin' for the National Guard."

Standing next to the Lighthorse cruiser, Katz tucked his thumbs into the front of his duty belt and gaped. "Phooo-*ooo*!"

"Oh, no," the woman said.

"She hit that thing full bore. She must be *butt*-wasted!" Katz bent at the waist and squinted at the truck. "It's a pure miracle that truck didn't go up in a fireball and roast her like a chicken."

The woman sucked in a lungful of smoke and began to cry. "Where do they come from?" she whined.

Bond said, "Deputy Katz, I think we've got a handle on this. That old wreck you passed on Bellwood just now? May be a crime scene. Guard it until OSBI gets there. And don't touch anything!"

Katz nodded while he continued to stare at the wreck. He smacked his palm with his fist. "Bam!" he said, and walked back to his cruiser.

Renaldo said, "Now, ma'am, I'm going to get your license and registration from the truck."

She wept quietly. She put her cigarette knuckle against one nostril and blew snot on the ground. Then she took another drag. "You really think I got a license?"

"Could I have your name, ma'am?"

"Tula Verner. Just like it sounds."

"I'll look it up." Renaldo walked back to his cruiser.

Bond asked the woman whether she wanted to sit on the grass.

She blew smoke through her nose and said, "Nah." Then she hung her head and sighed.

A lone buzzard gyred high over the wreck.

When Renaldo came back, he said, "Ms. Verner, this truck is registered to Douglas Verner. Is that your husband?"

"You'll find paper at the courthouse says that."

"Did he know you were driving the Ram?"

"I really doubt it. He was not around to ask his permission."

Bond said, "Jake, you want me to run her by the Mercy ER? By the time we get to the courthouse, you'll be done here."

"Thanks, Hannah. I'll inventory the contents and call Garn to tow the wreck."

Bond pulled handcuffs from her duty belt.

"Hold on there, cowboy," Verner said in a wet voice. "You're gonna put me in the hands of Mrs. Kong? Why don't you let me go with this cute Indian cop?"

Maytubby said, "The Chickasaw Nation uses the Pontotoc County Jail in Ada. We're in Johnston County. You have to go to Tish."

Tula Verner hung her head and crossed her arms behind her back.

CHAPTER 4

"Tempestuous Loves," Maytubby said.

"Violent Hates," Jill Milton said.

They were reading a framed lobby card for the 1949 movie *Tulsa* while they waited for a table at the Aldridge Hotel Coffee Shop in Ada. Susan Hayward and Robert Preston had stayed at the Aldridge while they filmed on location.

Jill tapped on the frame glass. "They don't mention insatiable greeds."

Maytubby moved his face closer to the glass. "I don't see any insolent prides."

They shook their heads. Jill said, "Not up to snuffs."

The greeter touched Maytubby's shoulder and pointed to a booth in the back. As his fiancée followed her, he felt the usual hush fall over the room. By the time he slid his campaign hat down the table, the place was noisy again. As she scooted into the bench, her thick black hair spilled over the lapels of her cobalt trench jacket.

She said, "Jay Silverheels was in that movie."

"Really." Maytubby looked at the menu. "I wonder if he ordered meatloaf."

Jill Milton shed her jacket and plucked at the shoulders of her wheat boyfriend shirt. She glanced briefly at the menu and slid it back behind the napkin dispenser.

"Speaking of Tonto," Maytubby said, "a woman Jake and Hannah and I roadblocked for DUI called me that."

"Probably an anthropologist."

"She's come to the right place. The Clear Boggy Valley is rich in colorful folkways."

Jill ordered a chef's salad without ham.

Maytubby ordered carrot salad and a boiled egg. The server knew not to ask. She pocketed her guest check pad and pen in her waitress apron and walked toward the kitchen.

Maytubby touched the back of Jill's hand. "Where did the nation's health forces join battle with Big Sugar this morning?"

Jill took a plastic tumbler of ice water from a busser and sipped it. "I was supposed to do the Eagle Play in Tupelo, but when I went to the warehouse this morning to get the props . . ."

"The healthy foods—plaster crooknecks and plums and such."

She nodded and wrinkled her nose. "There was a sewage backup in the office."

"Soooo you spent the morning washing fake zucchini?"

"Yessir."

Maytubby slipped the paper ring off his paper napkin. "Wearing your pantyhose?"

"Unless the Nation changed its dress code yesterday."

"I thought maybe there were contingency loopholes."

Jill pinched his campaign hat by the crown and wagged it in front of him.

"Good point," he said. She dropped it on the table.

His radio crackled. They looked at the table and waited. It fell silent.

Jill pointed at his shoulder mike. "I'm getting one of those. Stabilize the balance of power."

"Who's gonna call you?'

"Nutritionist Dispatch."

"Oh, yeah."

The server brought their food and left. A man in a Western hat and boots and creased jeans stopped at the table. A toothpick bobbed in his lips. He gestured at Maytubby's food with his check and removed the toothpick. "You know they serve food here. Right, Officer?" The man patted Maytubby on the shoulder. He glanced at Jill and looked quickly away before he resumed his walk to the register.

Jill ate a carrot stick with her fingers before she drizzled oil and vinegar on her salad. "Toothpick guy didn't know how black I am till he got close."

Maytubby forked his egg in half. "Have you considered he may have been startled by your radiant beauty?"

She watched the man in the Western hat open the front door. "When he was fake-mocking your food, I was thinking for one second I missed that kind of stuff when I was at NYU."

"And then he reminded you it can come with the other stuff."

Jill twisted her lips and nodded. She stabbed her iceberg.

Maytubby shook Flaming Lips hot sauce on his egg. "Hannah and I were called to a suspicious death on Pennington Creek this morning. Old allotment land. Guy in waders and fishing vest facedown in a pool. East of Mill Creek."

"Why suspicious?"

"Trout in his creel." Maytubby quartered his egg.

"Those are only in the Blue."

Maytubby nodded. "Car parked by the creek? Stolen Texas plates."

"Sketchy."

"That car? 1956 Hudson Hornet. No battery, no belts."

Jill munched a tomato slice and looked at Maytubby for a beat. "That's either four-star lamebrain or *X-Files*."

Dishes clattered in the kitchen. Maytubby ate a quarter egg. "Medical Examiner and OSBI are on the creek now. Hannah and I talked with the woman whose son found the body. Deborah Laber. And her young deaf son, who goes to OSD. You've done some work there?"

"Football, not diabetes. Nutrition Ed. staff talked to the jocks. We used an interpreter from the Nation."

Maytubby said, "Could you text me the interpreter's name and number later?" He finished his egg and looked out the window at Twelfth Street. "That boy seemed spooked. Hannah noticed it, too." He looked back at Jill.

"You think he can't tell his mother what he saw, because he was doing something he wasn't supposed to."

Maytubby stuck his fork in the carrot salad. "I do now." He took a bite and talked through it. "You never let me have an insight."

"You're supposed to be a man and fake it."

"Like say 'Exactly'?"

"Exactly."

"See?" he said. "I'll never catch up."

Something crashed in the kitchen, and the room was silent for a second, patrons trying not to rubberneck. "So what are you thinking the boy was up to last night?"

Maytubby rested his chin in his hand. "The Fenimore Cooper narrative? He was night-scouting. Watching for owls and coons, bobcats and deer. When he was supposed to be in bed."

"And the dirty modern narrative?"

Maytubby swiveled his eyes. "He needed solitude to spank the monkey. He was meeting a friend for whatever passes for sex at that age."

"Remote place for that second one."

"Way. So. The weather is mild. Are you game for what passes for sex at our age over at my rustic territorial home? You won't burn or freeze like ice."

"Are you trying to woo me with some old poetry again?"

"It's Sir Thomas Wyatt."

"I knew it. But there's still no shower. Just a Popeye's cup in a clawfoot tub. Come to my place."

"Do you have any radish butter?"

"Sergeant, I have radish butter for the end-times."

Maytubby donned his campaign hat. "I'll bring the rutabagas."

"Said no Mountie ever."

CHAPTER 5

Hannah Bond stopped her cruiser at a fork in the dirt trail. She picked up a civil suit summons from the passenger seat. It was issued to LeeRoy Sickles. He was being sued by Eliphaz Valentine. She cut to the end of the long directions. Satellite maps were still iffy in the sticks. Delaware Creek slid through culverts under the left fork. The right fork was Butcher Pen Road. Bond laid the summons back on the seat and took the right fork.

She drove slowly because the cruiser hit high center on grass between the tracks. Small limestone bluffs rose on her right. A roadrunner burst from the underbrush and legged it across the road, a bloody fledgling drooping from its beak.

She passed an abandoned structure built into one of the bluffs far north of the road. It was built with stone blocks and had slot openings. It reminded Bond of an artillery bunker. Maybe a far-flung artesian bathhouse from Bromide's resort heyday.

A good way beyond the structure, behind a barbed-wire fence with a gap gate, the walls of a small limestone quarry cut into a bluff. A few small blocks were stacked at the foot of one wall.

Butcher Pen Road angled past a stand of flowering persimmon trees. Bond checked her rearview mirror to make sure her catalytic converter hadn't started a grass fire. Around a tight bend, she stopped to read a sign. It was hand lettered in black Sharpie on a water-stained interior door propped up by green steel T-posts. A cross hovered above the lurching text:

HOLEY CITY #2. COMMING SOON.

Below, a stylized Indian arrow with feathers like fishbones pointed across Butcher Pen Road.

Bond followed the arrow and saw, about fifty yards into an unfenced field of greasegrass, a tall man standing at the lowered tailgate of a very old green pickup—possibly from the forties. A long shock of graying hair swung from the pickup window. A woman, or man, asleep or resting.

The man on the tailgate was hammering something—a chisel, maybe—into a block of something. The squat unfinished building closer to Bond was built of limestone blocks, so probably limestone. From this distance, the man's long white hair and beard made him look Mosaic. After a dozen strokes, he paused, raised his tools in the air, and brandished them at the sky like a triumphant warrior.

Bond shook her head as she drove on. "Nut."

One of her foster fathers, a later one than the bastard who murdered her little sister, had taken Hannah to see the passion play at the Holy City of the Wichitas. The nut's building did remind her of the WPA's rendition of Jerusalem in granite stones—Pilate's judgment hall, the mount of Calvary, the Holy Sepulcher. The shadowy chapel there, with its recorded organ music and a wall covered with miniature tin arms and legs and breasts pinned there by healed persons, had spooked her.

Bond passed the last landmark in the directions: a rusted car hood nailed to a fence post. Faint white letters fanned across it:

PUT YOUR STAMP ON HAMP.

Loose chat raked the cruiser's oil pan.

The unpainted single-story house sat atop a low rise. The house was small and pointy. Its rusted tin roof sheltered a small porch on one side and a boarded-up bay window on the other. The porch supports were turned, and there were carved ornaments in the molding. A rich person's house in territorial days. Like Maytubby's.

Bond parked in the yard under a large bur oak. She lowered her windows, looked and listened for dogs. All she heard was a crow. Watching the front door, she picked up the summons with her left hand and got out of the cruiser. The front door opened, and a wiry bald man in a T-shirt and overalls stepped onto the porch. He was wearing black glasses and cradling a double-barrel shotgun with antique hammers and a duct-taped stock. The gun looked to Hannah like a 10 gauge. A portable cannon.

A cigarette danced in his mouth. His body twitched as if he were bothered by insects.

Bond put the trunk of the oak between the man and her pistol arm. She laid her palm on the pistol and shouted, "Sir, lay that gun on the porch. Slowly. And back away from it."

He said, "Well," as he settled the stock and then the barrel on the warped planks. He spat out the cigarette and stomped it. When he stood up, he threw his torso back and flattened his palms on his kidneys like he had back pain. Bond came around the oak and approached slowly.

The man stared over her head. "Eehhh, goddamn," he crooned, then grinned and jiggled his glasses. "You bring me a lottery check, Tall Drink?" He raised his eyebrows and bugged out his eyes as he seemed to exaggerate interest in the paper Bond was holding. He stuck his thumbs under the bib of his overalls and ran them up and down. "'Bout as likely as polky-dot on a hook-and-eye Dutch."

Bond stood at the edge of the porch and looked up. "Are you LeeRoy Sickles?"

The man leaned toward her and put his hands on his knees. He was unshaven and smelled of stale sweat even from here. "I b'lieve I'm fixin' to wish I wadn'." He closed his eyes and laughed, "Hee hee hee."

Bond looked at his shotgun on the porch. Its swan-neck hammers were uncocked. She held out the summons. Sickles took it with his left hand and jiggled his glasses with his right. His neck and elbows twitched. He brought the summons closer to his face and threw his pelvis forward like a marionette. Then he walked like one, his knees bouncing up and down, around the porch. Bond could hear him muttering the strange Bible name while he pulled on his earlobe.

Sickles halted in front of Bond, rolled the summons savagely, and jammed it through the hammer loop in his overalls. "*Eliphaz?* I never seen that name before." He paused, looked across the field. Then an angry gleam came into his eyes. "It's that fuckin' Tiny." He looked down Butcher Pen Road the way Bond had come, and jiggled his glasses. "God told Tiny my east fence was on his land. He needs that hill for the place where Judas hung himself."

"That guy with the old pickup back there?" Bond said.

Sickles leaned down and pulled his overall straps taut with his thumbs. "I wish God would tell Tiny to stick his pecker in a Bush Hog." He bolted up and walked toward the gun. Then he stopped and turned to face Bond. He leaned back, stuck out his right arm, and pointed shakily down the road. "Tiny—what's his name . . . Elephant's Azz—he lives on rockin'-chair money." Sickles nodded slowly. "That's right, Tall Drink. The gum'ment pays him to be totally crippled. His back ain't worth a shit."

Bond looked at him.

Sickles raised his eyebrows. "Look like it to you? Him liftin' those limestone blocks?" Sickles sobered and got a faraway look in his eyes. His quaking settled. "Wonder where'd he get money to pay a surveyor." A shredded roller shade fluttered inside the bay window. Bond glanced at it and saw that it moved with the breeze. "Maybe that new woman I seen him with." Sickles's gaze broke. He scratched his head furiously, then looked at Bond. "Tall Drink, that man is crazy as a shit-house rat."

Sickles muttered curses as he spun around and stalked into the house. He left the gun on the porch, but Hannah backed all the way to her cruiser just the same.

When she passed the field of greasegrass, Tiny and his old pickup were gone.

CHAPTER 6

Maytubby saw Sheila through the glass security portal of Lighthorse headquarters. As he tapped in the code, she gave him a smile and an index-finger salute. He didn't respond. When he was inside, she gave him a quizzical look.

"What? Entering numbers. Male."

"Oh, brother." She rolled her eyes, then stared at the ceiling. "Chief wants to see you."

Through the glass walls of Les Fox's office, Maytubby saw his face over a monitor, washed in screen light. The nation's governor watched mildly from a photo over Fox's head. Maytubby noticed that the governor had lost weight.

Before Maytubby opened the glass door, he looked at the governor to see the reflection of Fox's screen. A large fish thrashed over the gunwale of a fishing boat. Maytubby knocked on the glass. The reflected screen changed instantly to the Lighthorse Police insignia.

"Bill," Fox said. He peeled a yellow sticky note from the edge of his monitor and held it out. "We have the victim's name."

Maytubby looked at the note and then at Fox. "Douglas Verner. I heard that name not two hours ago. Hannah Bond and I helped Jake Renaldo stop a drunk driver close to Pennington. Tula Verner. Her pickup was registered to her husband, Douglas Verner. She said he didn't come home last night." He looked back at the note and then at Fox. "Said he had a girlfriend in Tish."

"She said 'girlfriend'?"

"'Slut' is the word she used."

Fox nodded.

Maytubby looked at the faux bird-of-paradise plant next to Fox's desk. "She said she had fixed his wagon for good."

"Oops."

Maytubby raised his eyebrows and nodded once.

"She in Johnston County?"

"Hannah took her to Mercy ER in Tish first. Maybe a few stitches. Sheriff Magaw probably has her in lockup by now."

Fox looked at the Lighthorse insignia and nodded, turned back to Maytubby. "Give me a second. I'll tell Magaw about the husband."

Maytubby turned from the chief's desk and looked over the bookshelf behind it. A photo of Fox's wife, dour as a tintype Victorian. A certificate of appreciation from the Chickasaw Lighthorse Police Youth Academy. A gold plastic trophy of a breaching largemouth bass on a wooden base. Its engraved plate read "Lake Texoma 4th Place Co-Angler."

Distant static from Dispatch played over Fox's subdued talk. He accidentally hit the keyboard with his elbow, and the thrashing fish—a hog bass—was now held aloft by a grinning angler. Fox didn't seem to notice. He said into the receiver, "I've never heard that name on anybody. Can you spell it?" He jotted on a sticky note.

Maytubby checked messages on his phone. There was one from Jill Milton. "*You still my rutabaga man?*"

"*In spades*," he texted.

Fox hung up. He picked up the pad of sticky notes. "Tula Verner's already lawyered up. Magaw thinks just for the DUI. He'll tell her about her husband. If she doesn't already know. Benny has plenty of time. She'll be there another six hours." He looked at the pad. "Guy who brought in the lawyer and going the bond? His name is El-i-phaz Valentine."

Maytubby tried to look amazed.

"I thought I'd heard 'em all," Fox said. He summoned a photo of Valentine's driver's license. His height was listed as 6'5".

Though Maytubby might have heard of Job from his mother's mother, his *ippo'si'*, after his mother died he read the Hebrew Bible in college at St. John's, the same semester he read Aristotle. Eliphaz was one of Job's obtuse comforters. "I never heard of anyone named that," Maytubby said.

Fox shook his head, peeled off the Eliphaz note, and stuck it on his desk. "Douglas Verner isn't a Chickasaw citizen. If his wife did fix his wagon . . . well." He turned to his monitor, made a little raspberry when he saw the fishing show. With a few strokes, he found and searched the nation's database. "She's not a citizen, either. We'll see if an Indian suspect turns up. Feds and state already in the loop."

Maytubby nodded and paused a beat before he said, "Do you have the name and address of the Dallas fisherman who . . ."

"Lost his pants?" Fox grinned.

"He might have seen something."

"If Dallas didn't see somebody steal all his fishing equipment and both his license plates . . ."

Fox didn't move.

"It can't hurt," Maytubby said.

Fox sighed and spun in his chair. He ran his finger down the sticky notes on his monitor, pulled off one near the bottom. He did not hand it to Maytubby, because Maytubby could memorize things. "Dr.—he's a podiatrist—Dr. Patton Archerd. With a 'D' at the end. The plates were on a new Range Rover." He stuck the note back on the monitor. It fell off and fluttered to the floor. "No trips to Dallas, Sergeant." He swiveled and looked up at Maytubby, who wasn't budging.

"I remember that surname from the Dawes Rolls," Maytubby said. The rolls listed members of removed tribes who were eligible for allotments when communal tribal land was stolen by the federal government. Maytubby watched Fox as the news about Archerd's name sank in.

"What? You want me to look up the *podiatrist*?"

"I can do it in my office."

"Mmmmmm," Fox growled. He swiveled back around and again

searched the Chickasaw citizens. The blue circle spun on his screen. "Any day now."

Maytubby looked at the monitor over Fox's shoulder. The name popped into a blank field. Patton Boyle Archerd.

"I'll be damned," Fox said.

CHAPTER 7

Hannah Bond recognized the big granite chiseler from Butcher Pen Road when he came through the front door of the Johnston County Courthouse. He favored his left leg. He was walking beside a short man in a gray suit and red tie. The short guy carried a metal briefcase. Bond couldn't recall the nut's weird name. It was on the affidavit of service she had just given the county clerk. LeeRoy Sickles called him Tiny.

Was this the lawyer Sickles said Tiny couldn't afford? Bond had never seen him around the courthouse. He looked like a possum—tiny black eyes and a pointy pink nose.

Bond couldn't do nonchalance. She could walk to a bulletin board near the receptionist's desk and pretend to read bulletins. Tiny and Possum weren't here about Sickles's land. They were here about Tula Verner. Was she the "new woman" Sickles was talking about? Or was the new woman the person asleep in his ancient pickup?

When Tiny and Possum turned into the hallway to lockup, Sheriff Magaw passed them coming the other way, toward Hannah. He was looking at her. "Hannah. OSBI says the body in Pennington is Douglas Verner."

Bond nodded toward the jail.

"Yeah," Magaw said.

"What did she say?"

Magaw put his hands on his hips and looked out the single front window. "Not much. She's still pretty drunk. She was real mad and then started cryin'. Chief Fox told me what she said about her husband."

"Fixed his wagon."

"Uh-huh," Magaw said. "She got a lawyer fast. Not the usual bondsman from Madill."

Bond half extended her arm toward the hall and looked past Magaw. "I think you just passed 'em."

He turned to look, but Tiny and Possum had disappeared. He turned back to Hannah. "I better see what the fifty-cent counsel wants."

Walking to her cruiser, Bond saw Tiny's pickup parked in a handicap space. A blue "Disabled" placard hung from its rearview mirror. It was, she saw now, a Dodge from the late forties. A person as tall as she was, with long graying hair, leaned against the front passenger fender, smoking a cigarette. When Bond came around the truck, she saw that the hair belonged to Jimmy Nail. It had been a long time since Hannah last took him down, for breaking a ventriloquist's jaw at the Johnston County Free Fair. He must not have cut his hair since.

Nail gave her the side eye and smirked. "Deppity Dawg."

Bond stopped on the sidewalk. She rested her thumbs on her duty belt and looked over Tiny's pickup. She didn't need a refresher on Nail's face—its illegible black eyes, drawn cheeks, and fleshy lips. She did flick her eyes over his shoes. Loafers. Hogs. She briefly looked into the sky. Loafers. Ratty, but loafers. With a little gold bar on top. Bond hadn't seen a man wearing loafers for ten years.

When she reached the fair stage, years ago, Nail hadn't even squinted as he pounded the redheaded boy's face. The girl dummy lay jackknifed on the stage, spattered with blood. Witnesses said the ventriloquist had made a joke about Nail, who was smoking in the auditorium door. Bond had locked Nail's right biceps in her left elbow, snatched the back of his right hand down at his wrist. He gasped and tried to punch her with his left fist, but she pivoted backward, out of his reach. "Get down!" she said.

"Fu— *Aaaahhhh!*" She bent his hand more, and he turned pale.

"Get down or I'll break your wrist," she said evenly.

Nail dropped to his knees, and Bond cuffed him.

Now he held his cigarette away from his face and spat on the curb in front of Bond's feet. On the pickup dash, she saw a Phillips screwdriver and an unopened PayDay candy bar, a wooden-headed mallet, and a short chisel. What she could see of the bed was empty except for a legless upholstered armchair with its back against the bulkhead. And a little glinting something. A piece of broken glass? But it was red—and not jagged.

"Tiny ain't sellin' this priceless antique, Deppity." Nail leaned away from the fender and took a small wobbly step toward Bond. He exhaled smoke and said quietly, "If you tried to hotwire it some night, he might not know you was the law. He might shoot you with his black-powder fifty."

Bond looked past Nail, at the stone tower of the territorial bank on Main. She shook her head and turned toward her cruiser. Nail hawked and spat on the sidewalk behind her. He whispered a word she couldn't make out.

CHAPTER 8

At Lighthorse headquarters in Ada, Maytubby swapped the cruiser for his 1965 Ford F-100 bronze-over-white pickup. A week earlier, he had retrieved it from Able Body Works, where the techs had repaired the damage from a Bonnie-and-Clyde fusillade at the Greasy Bend bridge a few months back. He was waiting for one side-view mirror replacement from eBay.

At Dicus Apple Market on Constant Street, Maytubby picked up three rutabagas. He bought a Gala apple and a quarter pound of Kanza pecan halves for the half-hour drive to Pennington Creek.

* * *

The pony truss bridge was deep in shadow when Maytubby stopped just behind the spot where the Hudson had been before OSBI released it and Garn towed it to impound. Dan Scrooby from OSBI had informed Fox and Magaw that Douglas Verner's body had been taken to the Medical Examiner's Office and the state had completed its work at the site and released it. Maytubby had a second thought about parking just there. Sometimes, perps returned. He drove around a bend and off the road, slowly, into a stand of sumac.

Maytubby took a Petzl headlamp from the glove compartment,

slipped its straps over his head. From his duty belt, he took a pair of blue nitrile gloves and slipped them on. He walked back to the bridge. There was still enough light for him to see the spaghetti tracks leading through the bar ditch to the gap gate. White flecks of dental cast stone, left by an OSBI investigator, clung on the grass around the tracks. In the ditch, he could see the large shoe prints between the ruts, going in both directions. There were smaller shoe prints outside the spaghetti—probably OSBI.

The ditch mud told him the outbound cart, or whatever it was, was much heavier than the inbound. He went through the gap gate at the southern end of Deborah Laber's property, into a field of last year's tall bluestem grass. Dusk emphasized the paths of whatever was pulled through here last night. Still, Maytubby moved slowly, peering at the ground beneath the bent grass stalks. He saw nothing unnatural. Just before he came to the riverside brush and timber, he stopped and switched on the Petzl. A pattering rustle in the direction of the Laber house. Likely a whitetail.

Two more steps, and he found small knots of crime scene tape left on tree forks after OSBI had ripped away the rest when they were done. Behind the disturbed earth and leaves. Here the wheeled implement had been turned around. Good. The detective would have searched for blood. The tape remnants followed the trail of the dragged corpse toward the spot where Maytubby and Bond had turned back earlier in the day.

Now he stepped a few yards back from the old tape barrier and slowly walked parallel to it in the direction of the river. He scanned the dirt and fallen leaves, regularly turning his face and the light away from the trail, into the woods. Every couple of steps, he paused to listen. Up in the sycamore crowns, a great horned owl cooed, then screeched. Pennington Creek burbled in the near distance.

When he reached his earlier turnaround, he put the creek behind him. A field mouse scurried through the leaves. Maytubby moved his head to keep his light on it. A few yards away, the mouse halted and turned left. The obstacle came into focus—a sprung foothold trap for small game. He walked to it and squatted. It was an old one, like those Maytubby had run as a kid. An Oneida Victor. The chained stake that had secured it to the ground lay beside it, streaked with mud. Pinned between the jaws was a short, thin length of red plastic, like a bristle.

OSBI may have had bigger fish to fry.

Maytubby photographed the trap. From his duty belt, he took an evidence marker and a large plastic evidence bag. He stuck the marker in the ground next to the trap and photographed them together. Then he dropped the trap into the evidence bag and set the bag on the ground.

He walked slowly away from the tape and the bag, scanning the brambles and brush. A vehicle on Bellwood Road crunched shale as it slowed and stopped somewhere near the pony truss bridge. Maytubby couldn't see the headlights through the trees. The engine fell silent.

He walked in a widening zigzag. Soon, he saw no more investigator tracks. Between mature trees, he parted groves of saplings. His boots snapped on acorns. Spring was far enough along, he could almost have gone barefoot like the Mexican Tarahumaras he so admired. In another week, he would be taking his runs without sneakers.

A vehicle door slammed on the road. Maytubby stood still and switched off his Petzl. It was full dark now. The owl cooed again. Soon, Maytubby heard slow footsteps in the brush. A dim point of light appeared, swept the trees. He moved softly behind a sycamore trunk. The steps came a bit closer and stopped. Maytubby could see the faint light playing in the trees. Then the light settled on the ground a few yards to his right. He couldn't see what was there.

A male voice stage-whispered, "That little deaf shit." A zipper went up and down, up and down. *Zut. Zit. Zut. Zit.* "He don't show . . . huh. Get 'um." More footsteps. The voice again, nearer. "Okay, then." The person was now close enough for Maytubby to hear him spit and to smell his booze-steeped body.

Maytubby raised his left hand to the Petzl switch and set the heel of his right palm on the backstrap of his Beretta. He waited until he heard nothing from the man. Then he spun to his right and clicked on the lamp.

The man froze for an instant. His crimson eyes bulged under strands of greasy hair, and his toothless violet gums shone with tobacco juice. The hair on Maytubby's neck rose. The man's lips and patchy beard were stained with tobacco. He spun and bolted toward the road.

In the second it took Maytubby to put a name to the face—Raleigh Creech—Creech had run too far to chase. And he wasn't a suspect. For now. When Maytubby heard the rusted muffler uproar on Bellwood Road, the image of Creech's cratered Datsun pickup came to him from their last interview, in the Arbuckle foothills. Maytubby had been looking for Raleigh's sister's wanted boyfriend. Creech poached game, hunted out of season, and ignored bag limits. His truck was a rolling slaughterhouse. He had given Maytubby a good steer, but only because the suspect was an Indian, and Creech hated Indians. He had flipped Maytubby off as he drove away.

Putting Creech and the trap together, Maytubby was pretty sure of one thing Jason Laber had been doing in the woods. He walked to where Creech had pointed his flashlight. The Petzl soon revealed a primitive lean-to, its front loosely gated with chicken wire. He squatted, peeled back the wire, and looked inside. There were two shelves made of branches, built on tall legs to keep them well off the ground. The joining was all done with thin sisal rope. Maytubby duck-stepped closer. In the LED floodlight, six ringed coon tails glistened on the ends of pelt-stretcher planks. The skins they were attached to had been fitted, fur side down, over the tops of the bullet-shaped planks. Finishing nails held the skins taut, tails pointed straight down.

Maytubby admired the fleshing job. No trace of fat, and not a single nick. A bowed two-handled fleshing knife hung by one handle from the top shelf. A whetstone lay on one of the stretcher planks.

The season for most furbearers had closed a month ago. That wouldn't bother Creech. Was Jason afraid cops would find his pelts? Maybe he didn't know the game laws.

If Raleigh Creech didn't frighten Jason, what possibly could? Maytubby shook his head. If Creech had turned on Jason last night, he wouldn't have been expecting the kid tonight. Was Creech dragging a body scarier than Creech *not* dragging a body? Was the poacher connected to the abandoned Hudson? Had Jason's skins led Raleigh Creech to a promising stage for a fake murder?

Maytubby photographed the skins and took one with him. He replaced the chicken wire, stuck an evidence marker in the wire, and photographed the scene again. He captioned the photos with directions to the pelts and sent the photos to Fox, Magaw, and Scrooby.

Then he retrieved the bagged trap and its red bristle. He would deposit the bag and pelt at Lighthorse evidence custody, for OSBI, before he called it a night. His CLEET training required him to tote all the pelts to headquarters, to maintain the sanctity of the crime scene for the state. Trapper Bill. Nah. They missed 'em, they could find 'em.

He turned off the headlamp and stood in dappled moonlight. Some little beast skittered through the leaves. The running thing, when Maytubby came into the trees—was that Jason? Some faraway coyotes yipped. He looked up at the patches of sky untaken by the spring forest canopy. Rigel, ice blue, flickered between cottonwood branches. A mild south wind carried the scent of Chickasaw plum blossoms. He was suddenly famished for baked rutabagas and Jill Milton.

CHAPTER 9

When Maytubby stepped onto the long porch of his territorial gable-and-wing house, he saw a large white rectangular box beside the screen door. Its shadow oscillated as the naked porch light swung by its ancient wires. He bent to read the return address. The Deering Company. Spring Valley, CA. He left the box on the porch while he changed clothes.

The old house was drafty—cold in winter, hot in summer. In all seasons, it made a lot of noise. Springtime—except for late snows—was tolerable there, but Jill Milton disliked washing her hair with a Popeye's cup in his stained clawfoot tub.

Maytubby rinsed the young spinach he had cut in his garden that morning, laid it on half a kitchen towel, and folded the other half over to blot the leaves. In his bedroom, he placed his duty belt on the night table and hung his Lighthorse uniform on a wire hanger, which he then hung on a mounted cow horn his great uncle had given him. He buttoned a white Oxford shirt and pulled on gray slacks, an olive blazer, and a pair of brown Doc Martens. He draped a burgundy tie over the uniform.

He carried his uniform and duty belt to the pickup. He kept an extra pair of boots at Jill's. He returned to gather up the spinach and the white box. His campaign hat and the rutabagas were still on the pickup seat. He turned his hat over and dropped the rutabagas and spinach in the crown.

* * *

South Broadway climbed to Kings Road. Maytubby took a left. He drove between mansions built by the 1930s Fitts Play boom oil. Spanish colonial, Tudor, Georgian. They commanded a bluff overlooking the Clear Boggy valley.

Jill Milton lived in a garage apartment behind one of the mansions. Her great-grandfather, the son of a Chickasaw freedman, had lived there, above whatever luxury automobile he drove when he chauffeured the oil baroness in the big house.

Maytubby parked and loaded his arms with uniform, cap, and rutabagas. Then he changed his mind—dumped the rutabagas and spinach out of his hat and rehung the uniform. Donning the Smokey hat, he put his right arm around the white box.

As he climbed the stairs, he flashed back on a snowy morning several months back, when he held Jill on the landing and brushed splinters and snow from her hair. While Maytubby and Hannah were in a firefight with members of a rural crime ring down on the Washita, the gang's boss had gone looking for him and broken down her door. After she took out his knee with the freedman's old Springfield twice-barrel, he collapsed on her five-string Deering banjo and smashed it.

Jazz Night in America on KGOU drifted down from an open window. Maytubby took the last step, donned his hat, and knocked. "Package!" he said.

The porch light came on. Jill opened the door with one hand and held a fistful of apron in the other. Maytubby smelled the hot metal of an oven. She looked him and the package over. "I thought you were bringing rutabagas."

"Rutabagas are not very sexy."

"And?"

"I was trying to combine the brawn and transience of the delivery man with the authority and power of a lawman."

"You look like a goober."

"I didn't want you to think I take you for granted."

"Now, rutabagas might have gotten you laid."

"What do you think's in this box?"

"I'm pretty sure no rutabagas ever came in a white box shaped like a Boot Hill coffin."

"I have loose rutabagas in the truck." Maytubby said.

"I think the moment has passed." Jill sighed and made a fake sour face. She took a step back and held the door wider. He brought the white box in and set it on the floor. "I'm chopping onions," she said.

Maytubby went back to the truck and carried in his uniform and the food. He hung his uniform and placed the food on her kitchen counter.

He slid an inlaid cutting board the shape of Oklahoma from a bottom drawer and set it next to the board Jill was chopping on. He selected a weathered chef's knife from a top drawer.

"Half-inch cubes for the rutabagas," Jill said.

Maytubby sliced. "What state do you have?" he said.

She raked aside some onions and considered her board. "Hawaii." She chopped more onion.

Maytubby finished one root and raked the cubes to one side. "So you got wine that pairs with . . ." He sized up the other ingredients in Jill's ramekins and frowned. "Is that *cocoa*?"

"The wine savants said German Riesling. Riesling in the fridge. *Nicht* Mosel Valley."

Maytubby opened the cabinet above his cutting board and set out two wineglasses. "Clear Boggy valley."

"Our very own Waddell Vineyards."

"And wedding chapel," Maytubby said as he carried the bottle from the refrigerator to the counter. He pulled the cork with a waiter's corkscrew. "I hear they're building a rustic-events center behind the chapel."

As Maytubby poured, Jill said, "Locavores get their wine; rustic people get a place for their faro and reels. Win-win."

"You think it's fair to look down your nose at rustic people just because we have our own stomp grounds?" Maytubby stood behind her and set her glass on the counter. "Hey! That's not Hawaii."

"Hawaii, Wyoming. Get over it."

Aretha Franklin sang "Spanish Harlem."

Maytubby took a draw of Riesling and set his glass beside Jill's. He put his arm around her waist and rested his forehead on her hair. She laid down her knife, sipped some wine, and turned her face toward his. They kissed gently and long.

The windup kitchen timer interrupted them. Jill put her hand over it. "The stove is ready for your rutabagas."

Maytubby pulled out the drawer under the oven and slid out a cookie sheet. "What a sentence. Puritan sermon or soft-core romance novel?" He set the sheet on the counter and took a green bottle from the cupboard.

"I think once you oil 'em up, the die is cast."

He scooped the cubes with two hands and scattered them around the pan. "Even if I consign them to the fire?" He laced the rutabagas with olive oil, salted them, added a smidge of radish butter.

Jill took another sip of wine and peeled a garlic clove. "Yep. They'll sizzle."

Maytubby slid the pan into the oven. He twisted the timer face to zero and back to twenty.

Jill put her hands on her hips. "Okay, stud, what's in the box?"

"I told you. Fancy rutabagas and turnips from Harry and David. Individually wrapped in gold foil. The Royal Tuber Collection."

Jill walked to the box and glanced at the label. "Just in time. My picks were getting dusty." She walked back to the counter and shook a few tablespoons of toasted piñon nuts from a ramekin onto Maytubby's cutting board. "Nutcracker or hammer?"

"I usually use my teeth."

She took a hammer from her tool drawer and laid its handle in Maytubby's palm.

"You got any tweezers in there?" he said.

"You'll just have to whack the little suckers on the fly."

He corralled a few and gave them a gentle rap, picked the nuts out of their shells, and plinked them back into the ramekin. Jill pinched one at a time into the jaws of a lever nutcracker.

Maytubby squinted as he popped a few nuts. "I learned at least one of the things the deaf boy Jason does at night."

"So, dirty or Fenimore Cooper?"

"The second. And I mean. He traps."

Jill paused her nutcracker. "Really. Coyotes? Beaver?"

"The skins I saw were coons." Maytubby thumped a few more piñons.

"My grandfather Milton did that. He sold the skins to some business in Shawnee. I didn't think anyone still trapped."

"I did it. Some. When I was Jason's age. Nobody taught me. I read how-to books."

"What did you do with the pelts?" Jill swirled her wineglass.

"Hung 'em on my wall. Made me feel like a mountain man." Maytubby finished the piñons and brushed Jill's and his shells into the trash. "Tonight in the Labers' woods, I surprised a game felon who was looking for Jason. Neither of us saw Jason. You've never had the privilege of meeting Raleigh Creech."

"A game felon. Poaches, hunts out of season, exceeds bag limits. Like that?"

"All that and more. He sells venison from an ice chest in his pickup. Huck Finn's dad?"

"Pap. Yeah." She nodded.

"Raleigh Creech makes Pap Finn look like George Clooney." Maytubby pulled the stems off his spinach. He took two Silver Sage Frankoma bowls from the cabinet and distributed the spinach between them. From the ramekins, he pinched a few piñon nuts and golden raisins, which he sprinkled on the spinach. Then he set the bowls on Jill's drop-leaf table. He took a barbecue lighter out of the tool drawer and lit the candle stub on the table.

"Sounds like the kind of people who break down my door. He what, scared Jason?"

"I think Creech expected to meet Jason there. He was saying as much to himself before I showed myself. Then he ran off. My guess is, he was buying Jason's furs and taking them to auction. And coon season ended a month ago."

Jill lit a stove burner with the long lighter. She warmed a skillet for a short time, then coated it with olive oil. "Think Jason was afraid you and Hannah would find his pelts?"

Maytubby set the table with Frankoma plates that matched the bowls. "Could be. Or maybe somebody connected to the body in the creek threatened him."

"Like Pip in *Great Expectations*." Jill shook onions into the skillet. "Except Pip could hear."

Maytubby took the bottle of olive oil from the counter and poured some in a bowl. He grabbed a bottle of raspberry vinaigrette and whisked some with the oil. "And it's tough to read lips in the dark. Like snow is the blind person's fog."

Jill sautéed the onions, added garlic, currants, raisins, and shallots. "The presence of a dead body would do most of the talking." She added balsamic vinegar and deglazed the pan.

The oven timer clanged. Maytubby took some loop potholders from cabinet hooks and pulled out the rutabagas. He looked at Jill and then at the skillet. "Now?"

"Now." She stirred the rutabagas as he shook them out. She added piñon nuts, pumpkin pie spices, red chile, and cocoa powder.

Chick Corea and Bela Fleck were scorching a piano-banjo counterpoint when Jill turned out the overhead light and they sat down.

"I think there's a buckshot hole in this table," Maytubby said.

Jill raised her glass. "Here's to the freedman."

They clinked glasses and drank, spooned out the caponata. Maytubby said, "You got turnips or rutabagas in your collection of plaster veggies?"

"What do you think. We're trying to convince kids to eat something besides honey buns."

"Yeah," Maytubby said. "Slight chance turnips might backfire. My *afo'si* used to eat 'em raw, like apples."

"Your grandfather would have been a Depression kid."

"Instead of getting sick of them, he developed a taste. He also carried around a little bag of parched corn to break his molars on."

Maytubby ate some of the caponata.

Jill watched him. "And?" She turned her head and raised an eyebrow.

He stared at the ceiling for a second, then met her eye. "Healthy. It tastes *healthy*."

She nodded her head slowly. "Now you're for sure not getting laid." She drank some wine and ate a spoonful of caponata. She looked across the room and back at the table, then frowned at Maytubby. "'Healthy' is pretty vague, but I see what you mean. 'Peaty,' maybe."

"We could pour vodka over it and light it on fire."

"Rutabagas flambé!" she said.

They took quick bites and were soon working on spinach salad.

"I can't remember if Raleigh Creech has big feet," Maytubby said.

Jill canted her head.

"Oh. The shoe prints around the *X-Files* car were in clown territory."

"Clown in the woods at night might scare a kid," Jill said.

"In policeman school, we learned, when you hear hoofbeats, you shouldn't look for a zebra."

"What if the *X-Files* car was really tiny?"

Maytubby scraped leftovers into a casserole dish, gathered the plates and bowls, and sank them in dishwater while Jill blew out the candle and carried the wineglasses to the tiny coffee table. She switched on a gooseneck lamp by the sofa, picked up the library copy of Katherine Anne Porter's *Ship of Fools* they were reading to each other, opened it to the bookmarked page. Then she closed the book and laid it on the couch. "We're halfway through. Not exactly a parable of human goodness."

"Said the woman with buckshot in her kitchen table." Maytubby scoured the skillet, rinsed it, and put it in the dish drainer. He dried his hands and walked to the couch.

"All there in the title, too," she said.

Maytubby put his arm around her. "Can you read La Condesa's lines in that smoky Simone Signoret voice from the film version?"

She jerked her head toward the banjo box, tapped it with her toe, and clucked her tongue. "I will read to you, yez, if you promise to seat my resonator."

Maytubby reached over her and switched off the lamp.

CHAPTER 10

Hannah Bond swiped out of WhitePages.com and laid her phone next to her plate. She picked up her knife and fork and dispatched her meal of liver and onions. Pinched a heel of white bread, wiped juice off the plate, and ate the heel in three bites.

Her spartan hall-and-parlor cottage was silent. Before supper, she had cleaned her revolver. Hoppe's-#9-gun-oil fumes overpowered the smell of fried onions.

As she washed her supper dishes, she stared out an east window and watched the lights of trucks blustering into and out of Tishomingo on US 377. When the reflection of her flannel shirt in the window came into focus, it filled most of the pane. For some reason, the image brought to mind her friend Alice Lang, killed by a fellow bookkeeper who had embezzled from the Chickasaw Nation for the rural gang Hannah and Maytubby took down at Greasy Bend. Alice's killer was in Mac for life. He wore a long scar on his shoulder from the hatchet Bond put there at six paces.

Hannah lived alone and in herself. Alice, the finicky accountant who feared bridges—and who died on one—had come into Hannah's life when they worked at the Nazarene Food Pantry, handing out frozen wieners and peanut butter. Before Alice, Maytubby was her only friend. Hannah and

Alice went to John Fullbright concerts and shared *molcajetes* at Gonzales Restaurant. Alice's vile nephew, who claimed she and Hannah were "quar for each other," was briefly a suspect in her murder. He inherited her house.

Bond looked at her phone briefly, slid it into her jeans pocket next to her leather badge case, pulled on a Carhartt jacket, and slid her disreputable Smith and Wesson Model 10 service revolver into a jacket pocket. She was familiar with the stretch of Spring Creek Road where her phone placed Tula Verner's house. It was on a lonely stretch of the rock prairie—the Big Rock—not far from where Verner totaled her husband's pickup.

The lifters in Bond's old Buick Skylark clattered as she drove out of Tishomingo. Spring wildflowers played at the cusp of her headlights. Hannah Bond had no use for flowers.

She crossed the Blue River and drove beside barbed-wire fences anchored in rock-pile corner posts. South of Connorville, she turned west on Spring Creek—washboard dirt and red rocks across barren, stony fields. On her phone, the red place marker and her own blue dot converged. When the sodium yard lamps around the house appeared, she slowed to a crawl, rolled down her window, and turned off her headlights.

The Verner house was a brick ranch-style from the sixties, with no shrubbery and two satellite dishes on the roof. A single metal flagpole stood flagless in the front yard, the snap hooks on its halyard clanking in the breeze. There were no yard fences or dogs. Under a metal double carport in the lamplight, as she looked back she could see the rear ends of a new Cadillac Escalade and a new Nissan Titan. Both had dark paint and temp plates.

The Buick's cabin suddenly flooded with light. Bond hit her brakes before her eyes found the headlights motionless in her path. When the Buick came to a stop, the other headlights went dark. She switched on her own, which were reflected by the silver grille and ram hood ornament of Tiny's old Dodge pickup. Through its flat windshield, she saw the face of Jimmy Nail. His bee-stung lips and mesmerist's eyes.

The pickup pivoted in front of the Buick and pulled alongside it. Nail's window was down. He was now in silhouette against the Verners' yard lights. Bond's right hand slid into her jacket pocket and enfolded the grip of her revolver.

She heard the Dodge rev just before its rear wheels spun up rocks and sand that geysered over the Buick, rattling against her door and fender. A rock struck her left cheek, just below her eye.

She didn't touch the wound. The pickup's taillights shrank in her rearview mirror. "Maggot," she said.

If the lookout was done here . . . She turned off her lights and drove slowly west before stopping again. From the passenger-side floor, she hefted a huge pair of Steiner military binoculars. They were meant for a tripod, but in Hannah's hands they were like a toy.

She leaned out the window and rested her elbows on the run channel. The magnification forced her to hold the glasses very still. As she scanned the house and carport, she had to wipe blood off her left thumb. All the drapes and blinds were closed. She focused on the temp tags. Both said TEXAS BUYER. She balanced the Steiners on the run channel and typed the numbers into the Notes app on her phone. Beside these, she had just typed "Is Tiny in the" when the Verners' indoor lights went off and their porch and carport lights flashed on. She laid the glasses on the passenger seat and accelerated west, turning on her lights a way down the road.

At the top of the first hill beyond the house, a half mile away, a white Charger, its headlights off, edged out of a ranch drive hidden by a blackberry thicket, and blocked Spring Creek Road. As she braked, Bond checked her mirror. No headlights, no forms in the moonlight. Not that it mattered: the Charger was law. She looked at the driver to see what flavor. He wore a black shirt and jacket. Probably OSBI. Providing he was a cop. She laid her revolver in her lap.

The man got out of his car, keeping his right palm on his service pistol. He didn't look old enough to drive. With his left hand, he pulled out a badge case and flipped it open. "Oklahoma Bureau of Investigation!" he said. He put the case back and brought out an LED flashlight.

Bond slid the revolver back in her pocket and put both hands on the top of the steering wheel. As he walked slowly toward the Skylark, he held the flashlight in his left hand and kept his right palm on his service pistol. He stopped behind Bond's front door, briefly flicked his light over the Steiners, then put it back on her face.

Hannah said, "Agent, I'm Deputy Bond from the Johnston County Sheriff's Department. I'm armed. Commission card and badge in my left back pocket. Service revolver in my right jacket pocket."

The agent took three steps back and drew his pistol. He raised his flashlight over his head and kept it trained on Bond's face. "Exit the car with your hands up. Then turn around and put your hands on the roof."

Bond did as she was told. The agent holstered his pistol, reached into Bond's jacket pocket, and removed the revolver. He took a couple of steps back and laid it in the road. Hannah scowled at the dirt. The agent then patted her down. She could tell he was reaching up to get to her armpits. He pulled her cell and her badge case out of her back pocket and replaced the phone. Then he stepped back and said, "Raise your hands. Turn around to face me." She did so. "What happened to your eyes?"

"You saw those Steiner binoculars. Bumped the window post."

"Mm. Now slide down the car door and sit on the ground. Turn your palms up so I can see 'em."

As Bond walked her torso down the Skylark's door, her back smarted from a kick one of the Greasy Bend gang had dealt her on the Washita.

The agent tipped his flashlight, examined Hannah's badge and card. A kangaroo rat bounded from the bar ditch, landed between the agent's feet, and in one more hop disappeared behind the Skylark's fender. The agent didn't notice. He closed the case and held it out as he stepped toward Bond.

Hannah stood. The agent tilted his head back. She said, "Now you show me yours again. Up close."

He obliged her but didn't give up his flashlight. Bond turned the case so it caught light reflected from the Charger. Reed Cable. Agent I. A rookie. She handed it back to him. "Agent Cable." He didn't move to retrieve her pistol. "Could you get that light out of my face?"

He aimed it into the blackberry thicket. "Your sheriff—McGee. He's turned the Verner homicide investigation over to the bureau."

"Magaw," Hannah said.

"What?"

"The sheriff's name is Magaw."

"I know that, ma'am."

"And you forgot the Lighthorse Police and the FBI," Hannah said. "The body was in Indian country."

Agent Cable shifted his weight and deepened his voice. "I just want to know what a county deputy without their uniform is doing stopped in the road, at night, in front of the victim's house."

Hannah said nothing.

"I saw your name in Trooper Reynolds's report on the arrest of Mrs. Verner."

"Renaldo," Hannah said.

"Huh?"

"The trooper's name is Renaldo. Comes from Italian miners in Coalgate."

Cable shifted again. "Who was in the vehicle that stopped you down there?"

"One of my quilting pals."

In a few more weeks, there would have been crickets.

Hannah waited.

"What's her name?" Cable said.

"Wilma Handue. H, A, N, D, U, E."

Cable lowered his flashlight and turned toward his cruiser. She could hear him whispering the letters to himself until he got in. She lifted her revolver from the road, pointed it down, and slapped it against her palm to knock some sand out of the chambers.

Cable backed the Charger behind the blackberry bush.

Hannah stuck the pistol in her pocket and walked back to the Skylark. As she drove toward Tish, she imagined Agent Cable's boss, Dan Scrooby, reading his surveillance report, blowing like a whale while shaking his head, falling silent, and then looking at the rookie. "'Wilma Handue,' Agent Cable? Fiancé by the name of Jack Soffalot?" Cable still wouldn't get it. Scrooby would tell him he got hosed. Bond almost smiled.

CHAPTER 11

Jill Milton's sign-language interpreter connection, Fran Overton, was standing in front of the Chickasaw Nation Department of Language building when Maytubby steered his unmarked cruiser off Mississippi Avenue into the parking lot. It was empty except for a nation pool car and an older Honda Civic. Overton wore a navy skirt suit, black pumps, and pantyhose. Maytubby had added the burgundy tie to the blazer and slacks he'd worn to Jill's. His uniform hung from a garment hook in the back seat.

She slid into the cruiser. Maytubby introduced himself. "Thanks for coming out on short notice—and on a Saturday." He pulled back onto Mississippi and headed south.

"Dress code doesn't know about weekends." Overton turned her hand palm up and swept it to include them both. She didn't smile or frown. A pleasant face framed by a silver bob.

Maytubby nodded. "Or mud. Or the people we're talking to."

"You said it was a boy. A student at Sulphur. We're gonna scare him."

"I know. At least for me, it's better than the Lighthorse uniform." Maytubby joined the Ada bypass and briefly glanced at Overton. "His name is Jason Laber. And I think he's a lot more scared of something else." She didn't ask what.

Fran Overton said, "There's a code about interviews like this. You have to stand right beside me when you're talking to Jason. I can't tell you anything he might communicate to me in your absence."

"Really," Maytubby said. "I had thought he would warm to you better because you're not a cop."

"You were planning to let me conduct the interview, and then debrief me."

Maytubby skewed his lips. "Yeah, I was."

"Sorry." She looked out the window. "Also, in the interest of complete neutrality, I probably should have come in a separate car."

"Really. That's hard-ass."

Fran Overton nodded. "But considering we're going into darkest Johnston County . . ."

Maytubby smiled.

"Here's how we dance," she said. "While you're talking, I'll stand next to you, signing and speaking your words. When Jason speaks, I'll shift ninety degrees toward him. I won't go to his side, because I can't see his signing well. You will speak directly to Jason all the time—not to me."

Maytubby said, "By law, Deb Laber has to be present because Jason is a minor. But it would be better if we stood a ways from her and talked softly. Is that kosher?"

Fran Overton shrugged. "That's your bailiwick, Bill. How well does Ms. Laber know ASL?"

"Pretty well, I think," he said.

She didn't answer immediately. When he turned to face her, she was looking at him. "Oh," he said. "Not our voices, Jason's hands."

"Right. In my ninety-degree move, I'll try to stand between Jason and his mother so only you can see what he says."

She watched pecan groves and knots of grazing Angus through the passenger window as Maytubby described the crime scene and summarized the early investigation. She pulled a stick of lip balm out of her purse and knocked its butt against her knuckle, like a pack of smokes. Then she removed the cap and applied the balm. It was not clear that she was listening.

* * *

Jason Laber opened the ranch gate for the cruiser, closed it behind. Overton put her fingers to her chin to sign "Thank you," but Jason ran past the cruiser, down the dirt drive. As the car jolted toward Pennington Creek, Fran Overton said, "Does Jason read books?"

Maytubby parked and set the brake. "I don't know. I've never been in his house." He reached into the back seat and retrieved a clipboard, handed it to Overton.

She glanced at his questions a few seconds, lifted the query sheet and looked at a printed photo of the half-submerged body, nodded, and slid the clipboard back onto the seat behind her.

"Clipboard is scarier than our suits," Maytubby said.

"Yeah."

They got out of the cruiser and watched Jason go inside his house. "Before I picked you up, I phoned Deb Laber to give her a heads-up," Maytubby said. "Also told her about Jason's trapping and selling pelts."

"To the toothless guy who buys them. Raleigh Creech, who probably sells them for cheap hooch."

"Yes." It was a peculiar name. She *had* been listening on the drive over. "I'll reassure Jason that we won't rat him out to the game warden."

"I bet she was overjoyed her kid was out all hours trapping," Fran said.

"Ecstatic. I did tell her Creech's rap sheet was all poaching and that I would make him stay away. But also that she should keep her son inside at night for the time being. Jason kept the trapping a secret because his mom's afraid his deadbeat father, who lives in Flagstaff, will kidnap him."

"How do you know about trapping?"

"Deb Laber asked me the same question. It's something I did when I was his age, in the country. I read how-to books I ordered from fish and game magazine ads. These days, all that is probably online."

When Deborah Laber appeared, she was already wearing the black waist apron for her lunch shift at Sipokni West. Maytubby and Overton moved closer together as mother and son approached. Jason watched his own feet until he stood in front of them. Then he looked at Fran.

Maytubby introduced Deb Laber and Fran Overton. They shook hands. Jason watched closely. Fran made her name sign by swiping the last three fingers of her right hand across her forehead and then turning her palm outward. Maytubby recognized the "F" but not the flourish.

Deb and Jason both half-smiled. Deb said to Maytubby, "Her name is Smart."

Deb signed "D" and then spread her hands over her shoulders, made fists of them, and flexed her biceps. "Let me guess," Maytubby said. "Her name is Strong."

"Or Brave," Fran said.

To Fran, Deb said and signed, "Fran, this is my son Jason." His name sign was the pinky-dip initial "J" plus two finger pistols recoiling.

Fran nodded without smiling. She said to Maytubby, "His name is Quick." She turned to Jason and raised her right hand in the universal "hi" sign. She moved her hand to her heart and dropped her right index and middle fingers onto the same two fingers on her left hand. Jason signed "Hi" as well.

A chickadee whistled in the sycamores.

Fran Overton stood next to Maytubby. Facing mother and son, Maytubby said—and Fran signed—"Deb, we're going to ask Jason to step over by your car while we ask him some questions. Jason, you're not in any trouble from us." He smiled. "I don't know how your mom feels about trapping."

Jason glanced at his mother and raised one eyebrow. She gave him a mock stink-eye. He walked away from his mother toward her sedan, about thirty yards away. Deb Laber stood still and folded her arms.

Fran began the dance, standing next to Maytubby.

Maytubby said, "I trapped when I was your age. I've seen your coon pelts, and they're better than mine." He smiled. Fran delivered Jason's thanks without changing places.

Maytubby said, "Do you sell pelts to Raleigh Creech—the stinky man?"

This time Fran moved closer to Jason. He signed, "Yes. He gives me a dollar for every coon pelt. A boy at school does the same and got us to meet one night." He gestured toward the south. "On the road."

"Thursday night, before you found the body in Pennington Creek, did you meet Raleigh Creech in the woods?"

Jason snapped his right index and middle fingers down on his thumb and shook his head.

"Were you supposed to meet him the night after you found the body?" Maytubby asked. Fran finished his question just a second after he did.

Jason's fist nodded "Yes."

"Thursday night, before you found the body, did you run into anybody else in the woods?"

Jason flicked his eyes toward his mother and then signed, "Yes. I was checking my traps."

"Do you remember where the moon was when you saw this person?"

Jason signed "yes" and pointed to a spot pretty far down the western sky. "The moon shadows were long on the dead leaves."

Maytubby looked at Fran's face. She raised her eyebrows, nodded, and smiled faintly. "So. This month, that would mean pretty late," Maytubby said. "What happened when you saw this person?"

Jason began to sign very fast. Fran's brow creased as she interpreted. "I saw a light coming toward me, toward the west. I turned off my flashlight and hid behind a tree until the walker passed the tree. All I could see was lit by some lamp on the walker's arm. Or reflected from grass and dead leaves. Tall man, walking slowly." He cupped both hands over his chest and let them fall a little. "Like he was tired."

A hawk screeched as it rode thermals high above them.

"Could you see the man's face?" Maytubby said.

"No. But he had something light-colored on his head." Jason made fists on either side of his head and pulled them down. "A helmet, maybe. With a rooster comb or something on top. He was pulling something behind him." Jason signed, one hand pantomiming pulling a wagon. Then he shook his head, mimed pulling with both hands at his sides, and spelled out "cart."

Maytubby nodded.

Jason shook his head, signed "Bigger," and spread his arms out wide.

"Did you see what shape it was or what the wheels looked like?" Maytubby stole a look at Deb Laber, who was watching intently.

"Too dark," he signed.

"Could you see if there were any loops on the cart handles?"

"Too dark," again. Then he finger-spelled "But."

Fran said to Maytubby, "When he spells it out, it usually means 'However.'"

She turned to Jason and told him to continue.

"The moon reflected off shiny things on the cart. Like diamonds."

"A lot of them?" Maytubby asked.

"No."

"How long did you watch the man?" Maytubby said.

"Just a couple of seconds," Jason signed. "I must have made a noise—stepped on a branch or leaves—because he spun around and caught me in his light. I ran home."

"Did he follow you?"

"No."

"Thank you very much, Jason," Maytubby said. "You've been very helpful. If you think of anything else about the man, have your mom phone me. She has my card."

Jason turned, and the translator, her left hand on his shoulder, conducted him back to his mother. Deb Laber put her arm around him, and Fran Overton patted his shoulder before she spoke and signed, "Thank you."

"This man with a chicken head, pulling the cart," Deb said to Maytubby. "What about him? Did he put the body in the water?"

"We don't know. But Jason's information may be of great assistance to us." The stiff cajolery bothered Maytubby.

Deb Laber put her free hand to her forehead. It bothered her, too.

"You have my personal cell number. Call me anytime, day or night. We can manage the fence gate."

She knitted her brow, frowned, and nodded. Then she and her son turned away.

Without speaking, Maytubby and Overton got in the cruiser and bumped up the drive. She offered to handle the gap gate.

When she slid back into the Lighthorse cruiser on Bellwood Road, he noticed that her pumps were dusty and she had sticktights on her pantyhose.

They retraced Hannah's drive across the Big Rock last night.

Overton picked the sticktights off her hose, collecting them in her left palm. She lowered her window and tossed them out, then closed the window and rubbed her hands together to shuck the sandy residue.

The cruiser passed White Elephant Road and bumped over the Spring Creek culvert. Overton ran her index finger up and down the bridge of her nose.

"Who's Raleigh Creech?" she said.

"Small-time game poacher. Lives in the Arbuckle foothills. Filthy character. Hates Indians. At a pelt auction, he can net a buck on every coonskin he buys from Jason. Enough to buy a few handles of rotgut hooch."

"Jason wasn't afraid of *him*?"

Maytubby shrugged. "Scarce jobs in these parts for a kid that age."

Overton frowned and looked out the passenger window. The road turned washboard, and the cruiser vibrated.

"A *Little Princess* death cart?" Maytubby said. The washboard gave way to rocky sand, and the cruiser's tires tocked.

"Oookaaay," Fran Overton said.

"And the rooster comb on top of the helmet." Maytubby scanned corrals on the outskirts of Connerville. He cleared his throat and said, "Big guy. Tuba player for Trojans. Or Spartans." He puffed out his cheeks and fingered air-tuba valves with his right hand.

"I have no idea what you're talking about." Overton said.

Maytubby moved his air-tuba hand to the top of his head and splayed his fingers vertically. "That's where you see helmets like that. You know, with the crest thing sticking up. Marching bands—parades, football games."

"I—"

"Wait." He looked up at the headliner for a second, then back at the road. "Tuba players can't wear helmets."

"Huh?"

Maytubby raised his hand and flapped it over his head. "The bell. The

Sousaphone bell. It gets in the way. Tuba players have to wear berets." He put his tuba hand back on the wheel and shrugged. "Ehhh. Big guys can play any instrument."

Maytubby stopped at US 377. He and Overton looked for oncoming. "Probably not a flute," he said. A mile north of Connerville, when they crossed the Blue, he said, "Or a piccolo."

CHAPTER 12

Hannah Bond and Eph split a Saturday shift for Katz so he could go to a Monster Truck Jam matinee in Oklahoma City.

Midmorning, she parked her cruiser between pickups in the Sooner Foods lot on East Main in Tish. The Byrd Street address Dispatch had sent her to, on the next block, hadn't rung a bell. But the hair-curling obscenities came from the right quarter. Man's voice. Grocery patrons just emerging from their vehicles flinched at the ruction. When they looked to Bond, she frowned and nodded as she adjusted her duty belt and walked slowly toward the neat 1960s neighborhood.

Waiting to cross Main, she looked down the alley that passed behind the Dispatch address, and saw the rear end of a white Charger parked in the middle of the block, its driver seated inside. How did the OSBI rookie hear about this?

A man rode a lawn tractor around his large lot, topping dandelions and henbit before the real turf awakened. Nearer the yelling house, Bond saw a couple of neighbors standing outside, peering through shrubs in that direction. The first ones to acknowledge Bond looked relieved. They walked quickly into their backyards.

Bond heard no signs of a struggle. She could see that the windows of the little ranch house were open. The door was slightly ajar. As she neared the porch step handrail, she heard the man shout, "You nasty *cooze*! *Whore*-dog!"

She paused and listened.

"I wouldn't of even got to the city *limits*"—the man's voice shot into falsetto—"and you were *peelin'* outta the driveway. You couldn't *wait*!" The lawn tractor muttered in the background. "Not five minutes. Not *three*! Just a filthy wrigglin' bitch in heat." His voice broke, then came back even louder, almost disembodied. "But he wasn't *there*, was he? At Nod Inn? Where was he? Where is he *now*?"

A woman's gasp fetched Bond onto the porch and through the front door. The man and woman stood at opposite ends of a small, tidy living room. The room smelled faintly of cigarettes, though there was no smoke. Bond had never laid eyes on either of them. The man fell silent. Both he and the woman stared at Bond.

Even bowed at the neck by rage or grief, the man towered over the room. His face was pale and damp, his thick hair matted. Hannah saw no weapon. She noted his button-down collar and black slacks, put them together with "the city limits," and pegged him for a salesman, even as she turned her attention to the woman who was likely his wife.

Wait. Bond looked back at the man's slacks. They broke, at the cuff, over a pair of boat-size loafers. With tassels. Then Tula Verner's words came to her: "that city slut in Tishomingo."

Bond stuck her thumbs in her duty belt and faced the man. "What's the bellerin' about, sir? You're spookin' the neighbors."

The man flicked his eyes to the nearest window, as if the truth might frighten him. He crossed his arms and looked at the floor. "It's personal, sir. I mean ma'am." He fish-waved a hand. "Officer."

"If it's so personal, Mr. . . ."

"Fenton."

"If it's so personal, Mr. Fenton, why are you callin' the hogs?"

The man stared at Bond. When he found his voice, he said, "This is—"

Bond halted him with her hand. "Stay put there, Mr. Fenton. I need to talk with your—this lady—alone for a minute."

Bond walked backward until she stood beside the woman. “Ma’am, let’s step to the north window here.” Bond shut the window and closed the drapes. The woman’s face was flushed. She panted and shredded a paper napkin. Bond lowered her voice almost to a whisper. “Turn and face the window while we talk. I have to keep an eye on the barker.”

The woman nodded as she about-faced.

“Is Mr. Fenton your husband?”

She nodded again.

“Has he ever hit you, Mrs. Fenton?”

“No.”

Bond took a business card from a back pouch in her duty belt and passed it to Mrs. Fenton, who dropped the last shred of napkin on the floor and took the card.

“Is he threatening to hurt you?” Bond watched the husband, who rubbed the back of his bent neck.

“No. He’s never acted like this. I think I’ve made him sick.” She glanced at the card and then whisked it behind her back. “The handwritten number is—”

“My cell. How would you make a big man like that sick?” Bond turned her head and looked down at Mrs. Fenton, who had spread her fingers over her forehead. Chestnut hair fell around her face.

“Some busybody told him I was seeing a man. Which I am. But now, that’s between Curt and me.” She dropped her hand, briefly canted her head backward, in the man’s direction. “I didn’t think he even knew those words. Is his face still white?”

“As starch.”

Mrs. Fenton said a little louder, “He’s gonna puke, Officer. Can I get him to the bathroom?”

Hannah stepped back and tucked in her chin. “Uh. Okay.” She spread her palms.

Mrs. Fenton walked quickly past Bond to her husband, who had put his hands on his knees. She grabbed his elbow and pulled. “Let’s go, Curt.”

He leaned toward her as they slowly stepped into a hall and disappeared. Soon, Hannah heard him retching and groaning. A toilet flushed, a tap squeaked, and water spattered. There was more retching. Hannah paced the living room slowly. Magazines stacked neatly on the coffee table next to a glass bowl of pinwheel mints. Remotes arranged by size, a few bestsellers in the bookcase. No Christian books she could see. The inside air, except for a whiff of smoke, smelled flowery.

The toilet flushed again. A tap squeaked opened and closed. Bond thought she heard Curt Fenton say, "Axe." She walked to the north end of the room so she could see the hall. A few seconds later, Fenton and his wife walked slowly past the open door, toward the back of the house. He was bent almost to the level of her head and had his arm around her.

A wren sang from the street trees. Bedsprings scrunched, a door closed, and Mrs. Fenton reappeared, kneading a hand towel. She draped it over the back of a ladderback chair. "He has a migraine," she said.

Bond looked past her, into the hallway. "You got it?"

Mrs. Fenton made a fake grimace and lowered her head. "I think so."

Bond nodded and walked out onto the porch. She closed the door behind her, stood and listened for a while. A wren sang; the tractor muttered. Mrs. Fenton sobbed.

When Hannah crossed Main, the Charger was still parked behind the Fenton house.

In the Sooner Foods lot, one of the pickups she had parked between had been replaced by a second white Charger. When Bond got to her cruiser, Agent Cable's OSBI boss, Dan Scrooby, lowered the driver's window on the Charger and motioned Bond over.

She didn't go over. She stood in front of her car and tucked her thumbs into the front of her duty belt. Scrooby exhaled loudly, opened the door, and grunted as he rose. He wore chinos and a black polo shirt with an embroidered badge over the left pocket. OSBI had banned the cross-draw holster he once wore under a jacket. Now his Heckler and Koch nine rode his ample hip in a molded belt holster. He left the Charger's door open, donned some aviators, and walked toward Bond. She stepped back from her car so Scrooby would have to stand in her shadow.

"Agent Scrooby," she said.

He put his hands on his hips, looked down Main for a few seconds, then up into Hannah's face. "*Wilma Handue*, Deputy Bond?"

Hannah stared over his shoulder at the Sooner Foods sign.

Scrooby blew through his lips and again tilted his head back. "OSBI has this case until there's proof the actual murder happened on tribal land and both the victim and perp were Indians. Don't you have shoats to chase off the road, or something?"

She now looked down at him. And frowned. "Why didn't your rookie intervene in the domestic? He had to be listening to the mutual-aid frequency."

He was silent. Bond saw her warped face in his sunglasses just before he lowered his head, twisted his lips. "He wasn't," Scrooby grumbled. "He's surveilling Curt Fenton."

Bond nodded. "Not about to blow his cover for a domestic."

Scrooby didn't move. Grackles pecked the asphalt.

"Same reason he didn't park right in *front* of the house."

Other grackles pecked the asphalt and grackled.

Scrooby crossed his arms and rocked on the balls of his feet. "So was Mrs. Fenton in any real danger?"

Not missing a beat, Hannah said, "If you think Curt helped Tula fix her husband's wagon, then get a print of his loafers." She stepped toward her cruiser door and left Scrooby standing in full sun.

After she opened the door, she said to his back, "They have tassels."

CHAPTER 13

From the Department of Language building, Maytubby drove a half hour south to the Chickasaw Travel Stop on I-35. He carried his uniform inside, took some friendly abuse for being a fancy pants. He changed in the back room and bought some buffalo jerky and raisins.

Back on the road, he crossed the Washita, swollen and muddy from spring rains. East of Davis, he turned south on the Dougherty road and wound through the Arbuckle foothills. He crossed the path of an old wildfire—blackened cedar skeletons and incinerated mobile homes.

Too long before he got to Raleigh Creech's house, he could see the poacher's yellow Datsun 720 pickup. Buzzards wheeled above the house in the noon sun.

When Maytubby pulled into Creech's drive, the poacher's back was turned toward the road. He was dressing an animal carcass that hung by a chain from a low cedar branch, its hind legs splayed by a rusted gambrel. Creech wore a ragged yellow T-shirt, with his greasy hair roosting on his shoulders. He stood barefoot in a pile of guts. A half-empty handle of clear liquor leaned against a rock at the edge of the shade.

The cruiser's tires snapped on chat, and Creech spun around, a bloody fixed-blade Case knife raised in his right hand. When he squinted into the sun, his upper lip rose and showed his toothless upper gums. The front of his shirt was roped with dried blood and tobacco juice. Hounds bayed from pens somewhere beyond crags of junk.

Creech shaded his eyes with the fist of his knife hand. As Maytubby got out of the Lighthorse cruiser, Creech rolled his eyes and spat, threw his arms in the air. “This here’s a legal wild hog!” he said, now pointing with the knife. “I got papers . . .” He spun uncertainly, tried to stick his knife in the carcass and missed, regained his balance and hit his mark. He began to dig in his hip pocket, pulled out some shreds and shook them at Maytubby. “The landlord got me permission to night-shoot. He put the ’lectric collar on the Judas pig and showed me how to use the other thing to follow ’im to the sounder. I done everthang legal.”

As Creech advanced with the papers, the stench of booze, old sweat, and guts rolled over Maytubby. “Mr. Creech,” he said, “I—”

Creech stopped in his tracks. He lowered his hands and leaned forward. “Wait just a goddamn minute. You ain’t no game law.” He overshot his center of gravity and stumbled forward.

Maytubby said, “No—”

“You’re that fuckin’ Indian cop came lookin’ after my sister. I gave you straight dope on her cranker redskin boyfriend.” Creech raised his right hand and then pointed in the direction she had gone years ago.

“Yes.”

Creech lowered his hand and pointed at Maytubby with his index finger. “This ain’t tribal land, Chief.” He shook the paper shreds at Maytubby again. “And neither is this. This is white people’s business. You got no reach here.”

“I’m not here about the hog, Mr. Creech.”

“I ain’t been on no tribal land.”

“In fact, you have. The deaf kid you’ve been buying pelts from? His family still owns the original allotment.”

Creech’s eyes bored into Maytubby. “Show me proof where I bought pelts.”

“I’m not here about the pelts. And the boy didn’t snitch. That was me in the woods. That was my old Ford pickup parked on the road.”

Creech raised his right arm and wagged it back and forth, knee-dipping like a dancing toddler. "Well, ain't that sweet. You drove all the way out here to talk sweet to ol' Rawl." Then he abruptly stood still and spat. Maytubby noted his small feet.

"The boy's folks don't want you on their property."

Creech looked past Maytubby, acting bored.

"It's also a crime scene. A body was found in Pennington Creek. Place crawling with cops—state, feds, tribal."

Creech shrugged, but Maytubby noticed him stiffen.

"You see that body?" Maytubby looked at Creech's face. "Ol' Rawl."

Creech's head snapped forward. The veins on his neck bulged, and his fingers writhed.

But this time he said nothing. Murder was not the same as poaching.

Maytubby took a Lighthorse contact card from his shirt pocket, showed it to Creech, and wedged it in the fork of a hackberry branch. "Call us if you remember anything weird around Jason's place."

Maytubby got into the cruiser, made a U-turn, and drove slowly down the drive. He looked in his mirror. Creech didn't flip him off like last time. Instead, he stalked back to the pig carcass, kicked the mound of guts, and pummeled the loins with his fists.

CHAPTER 14

"People see us leaving out of Tish in your Skylark together, there's gonna be talk." Maytubby carried his uniform through Hannah's kitchen on the way to his cruiser. He registered the banana scent of Hoppe's gun oil.

She had already changed into khaki pants and a black twill shirt. She gnawed a drumstick at her sink, watching the market-day traffic on 377. "Don't flatter yourself."

Maytubby laughed as he eased the screen door shut behind him. Not letting the single spring bang it shut was part of his country manners. He hung the uniform in the cruiser and laid his duty belt on the old Skylark's trunk lid.

Hannah tossed the chicken bone in the trash. She picked up a baked red potato and a saltshaker in one hand, her duty belt in the other. Just inside the screen, she put the potato between her teeth and held it in her mouth while she salted it, then set the shaker on a metal stool. She stowed the duty belts in the Buick's trunk. Before she slammed the lid, she took out a faded baseball cap that said "89ers," and pulled it over her eyes. "Hey, Bill, you want a secret-agent disguise hat for Dallas?"

Maytubby tossed a water bottle and the jerky and raisins onto the Buick's front bench seat. "Sure."

She rummaged in the trunk and found a cap for Quanah Cottonseed Hulls. Its logo was a generic male Plains Indian in a war bonnet. Maytubby held it by the bill and looked at the logo. "Thanks a lot, Hannah." He snugged it over his hair. "Render me invisible to the Highland Park rent-a-cops." He took the cap off and dropped it in the car.

After the Skylark shuddered to life, Bond flipped on her wipers and washed pine pollen off the windshield. She ate the potato while she took streets that were as far as possible from the courthouse. At the edge of Tishomingo, she waved at Eph, who leaned against his cruiser and pretended to clock the Buick with his radar gun.

They crossed the Blue River, then followed it south toward the Texas line. Faint spring pastels washed over the russet Cross Timbers country.

Bond rolled down her window and propped her forearm in the frame. "Strangest domestic I ever worked, in Tish this morning," she said over the wind. "Woman was the 'city slut' Tula Verner said her husband was seeing. Somebody snitched."

Maytubby cracked his window to cut the baffle. "How was it weird?"

"Not the screamin' part. The husband—name's Curt Fenton—did *his* job." Bond stared at the road a few seconds. "But his face was fish-belly white, not red. She'd hurt his feelers. And she was sorry for it."

"Not afraid-fake-sorry," Maytubby said.

"Right." Bond turned to Maytubby. "She took him to the bathroom 'cause he had to puke."

Maytubby said, "So you just stood around in the living room?"

"Pretty much."

"That is strange."

"Fenton does have big feet. And he wears loafers. OSBI's sweet on him. Scrooby's having him tailed."

"Where was the tail when you answered the domestic?" Maytubby said.

Hannah nodded, looked at him. "Parked in the alley behind the house."

"Rookie." Maytubby smiled.

"Rookie," Hannah said. "I thought he was going to shoot me last night. I surprised him when we were both watching the Verner house."

Maytubby peeled open the buffalo jerky and bit off a hunk. “Anything?”

“Two brand-new vehicles. Cadillac Escalade and Nissan Titan. Texas temps. Said ‘Texas Buyer.’ ”

“Good catch for night.”

“Steiners.” Hannah pointed her thumb at the back seat.

“Oh, yeah.” Maytubby nodded.

“Ran the numbers. Same dealership in Plano. Sitka Auto Ranch. Registered to a person named Ella Bednar.”

Maytubby frowned. “Bednar and Sitka. Czech names. Lot of Czechs in Texas.”

When the highway intersected Nail’s Crossing Road, they fell silent and turned to look down it, toward the old ford on the Blue where they had taken down the cunning hit man Hillers.

“Speaking of,” Hannah said, “Tula Verner’s mixed up somehow with this hoser named Jimmy Nail, sidekick of a big galoot named Tiny.” Maytubby watched Hannah place her forearms on the wheel, leaving her hands free above. She said, “Tiny’s building a copy of the Holy City, southeast of Bromide off Butcher Pen Road.” She mimed a mallet striking a chisel, raised her brows. “Outta limestone. Which he loads in an ancient Dodge pickup.”

“Took Roosevelt’s WPA to build the first one.” Maytubby shook some raisins into his palm and considered them. “And, really, another Holy City? The one in the Wichitas lost its tourist mojo before we were born.” He tossed back the raisins and swigged some water.

“Already a ghost town when somebody took me there as a kid.”

“The galoot—Tiny,” Maytubby said. “His real name Eliphaz?”

“It is.” Hannah looked surprised. “He known far and wide?”

“Fox told me he brought in a lawyer for Tula Verner.”

“I don’t get that,” Hannah said. She spread her right hand and held it between herself and Maytubby. “Let me go back.” She put her hand back on the wheel but gestured with her index finger. “This Tiny guy is trying to get some of his neighbor’s land for the Holy City. The neighbor, LeeRoy Sickles, told me that Tiny’s on Social Security disability. That he’s broke and crazy. I verified the disability. The others, I don’t know.”

Maytubby flattened the little raisin box and slid it in his pants pocket. "He's on SSD, he shouldn't be able to cut limestone or hire lawyers."

In downtown Durant, Bond stopped for a red light next to the monument for the World's Largest Peanut. She pointed to the yard-long granite peanut on top. "I heard there's a lot bigger ones."

"Stands to reason," Maytubby said.

"So what'd your sign-language girl learn from the deaf kid?"

"Jason Laber. Before Jason found the body, he saw a big guy—not Raleigh Creech, the guy he's selling pelts to—"

"Old Stinkbait," Bond said.

"Pulling an empty cart toward Spring Creek Road. Because we're ace trackers, we knew all that. But Jason said the big man wore a helmet with a rooster comb on top. And that the cart had diamonds—as in jewels—on it. The guy was wearing an armband flashlight and caught Jason in the light before the kid ran away."

Hannah looked at Maytubby. "Scarier than Raleigh Creech, you say."

"He might have been most scared of his mother. She doesn't allow him out at night, because his father has threatened to kidnap him."

"Wh—?"

"Flagstaff. And Jason's never laid eyes on him."

Hannah nodded. "And you've made the marching-band list."

"Trojans seven, Spartans two," Maytubby said. "But you can buy all that band stuff online now."

"I'm guessin' not. Thieved or dumpster."

"Yeah. Me, too." Maytubby tapped the dash. "One seventh of the Trojans go to Oklahoma Baptist Academy. Sportswriters call 'em the Oklahoma Baptist Trojans."

"Free advertisin'," Hannah said.

They crossed the Red River, passed a Texas welcome center, and drove through rolling pastureland north of Dallas, the fencerows greening up as they moved south.

Sitka Auto Ranch glinted between box stores right off Plano's artery, US 75. "Right on the way between Dallas and Tish," Bond said.

The highway took them all the way to Highland Park, where Bond exited on Mockingbird Lane. They passed the Dallas Country Club and a Moorish Revival shopping complex.

"Next left," Maytubby said.

They slid through a live oak canopy, between Tudor and Georgian houses. The feeder street opened into a large plaza bright with fountains.

Bond stopped under an entrance archway that said FOOT KINGDOM. She let the Skylark idle. The Gothic stone building across the plaza bristled with spires, pennants snapping in the breeze. "Damn," she said.

A pointed arch opened through the building's facade into a courtyard packed with SUVs. "Hot biscuits, Hannah, this joint's open on Saturday."

Bond nodded. "Yeah," she pointed. "I park in there, Missy's gonna call security."

"Let's see." Maytubby snugged the Quanah hat over his thick black hair.

Bond inched between the fountains and into the building's shadow. When the Skylark broke into sunlight, a muscled, blond young man in uniform held up his hand. Bond stopped. He looked at the back of the car and said something into his shoulder mike. Then he stepped to Bond's window. She lowered it, and the guard leaned over and smiled. He said, "You new?"

"Yeah," Hannah said.

He nodded. "Just drive straight through the lot and make a left at the groundskeeping shed. Parking in front. Supervisors are in there."

As Hannah pulled slowly away, she said, "What'd I tell you. These hats, they'll never think we might be cops."

"Looks like they're going to get us a job, too. But I think Officer Buff told Groundskeeping one of us is an Indian."

Only one other vehicle was parked in the groundskeeping lot—a black Nissan Taxi passenger van. White Roman letters on the driver's door read "Gautier's Non-Emergency Medical Transportation." Bond got out of the Skylark and walked behind the van. She pointed at the license plate. "Sitka," she said to Maytubby as she joined him. Maytubby took out his phone, turned around, and photographed the front Texas plate.

Scarlet azaleas flared along the sidewalk into a green shed blanketed by confederate jasmine. When Maytubby and Bond walked in, they faced a ruddy, wet-eyed man of about sixty, haphazardly shaven and wearing a stained linen sport jacket. He held two sheets of paper in one hand and two sharpened pencils in the other. The paper trembled faintly.

The three stood silently for a few seconds. The wet-eyed man cleared his throat and looked sideways out a window. "Dr. Archerd is in charge of the grounds. As you know, our landscape associates receive free podiatric care. That's foot care. When you have filled out your applications, you can go. A supervisor will take them to his administrative assistant. She will contact you soon."

He extended his pencil arm toward a round Formica table and four fiberglass chairs. When Bond and Maytubby were seated, the wet-eyed man laid the applications and pencils in front of them and went outside.

Maytubby took out his cell and photographed one of the forms and the room.

A small speaker high on the wall played easy listening very softly.

"Minty-fresh breath," Maytubby said. He picked up his pencil and bent over the application.

Bond stared at him until he chuckled and looked at her. She spread her arms to indicate the whole room and then pointed to her application. She said, "What the hell *is* all this?"

"Don't you ever go to the podiatrist, Hannah?"

She smacked her lips, then ironed the application to the table with a palm and raised her pencil. "All right, smart-ass, what's our job history?"

"No place on here for addresses of former employers or references. Pretty good chance they don't care. I'm going to put 'learned astronomer.' "

Bond slapped the paper. She pointed straight ahead with the pencil and then pivoted in her seat. "You see a single tool in this place?" She pointed down. "Not a blade of grass on the floor. I call bullshit."

"Not a garage—or even another shed—on the property," Maytubby said. He bent to his application.

A few seconds later, they looked at each other. Bond said, "My address is already printed on here: a P.O. box in Gainesville, Texas.

"Mine's in Sherman."

"Both right up on the state line," Bond said. "Yours also have a 'may be found at' address?"

"Yep. And the blank for the Medicare Medicaid 'referral.'" She made air quotes around the word.

Easy-listening oboes fogged the cool, dark room.

"Our own cell numbers?" Maytubby said.

"What I put," Bond said.

They photographed their forms with their phones.

The front door swooshed open, throwing light and jasmine into the room. Maytubby and Bond turned and saw a different man. Midfifties, tall and muscular, with close-cropped blond hair going gray. He could have passed for the entry guard's father, minus the smile. He wore a dark print sport shirt snug around his biceps and pecs. It had a spread collar and rolled short-sleeve cuffs.

He walked slowly to a window, his back to the table, and bumped his fists against his thighs. A few seconds later, he sighed, walked to a small black electronic device mounted below the speaker, and touched it. Country rock erupted. Maytubby and Bond looked up, and the man looked them over and shook his head slowly. "Time's up," he said, extending his hand toward the table. Maytubby and Bond handed him their forms and left the pencils on the table. He glanced at the paper and raised his eyebrows. "They can read *and* write," he said softly.

He rolled up the forms and turned toward the door, muttering.

"Hey," Maytubby said. The man stopped and half turned his head. "We fixin' to meet the doctor?"

The man turned full about. His face was hard and heavy-lidded. "Mr. . ." He unscrolled the forms and read. " . . . Whitman." He looked at Maytubby. "The doctor has gone home for the day. One of his assistants will contact you." He rolled the papers up and held them in the fist he used to bang open the door.

"Steel-toes, size fourteen at least," Hannah said.

Maytubby rose. "Archerd's a big dude, too. Saw him on the website. What's your alias?"

"Same as I gave Scrooby's rookie. Wilma Handue." Bond leaned over the table and pushed herself up.

Maytubby snorted.

The medical transit van was gone, replaced by an aqua 1957 Chevy short-bed pickup.

Bond cranked the Skylark while Maytubby touched Google Maps. Watching the screen, he said, "Go back over the drawbridge; make a left."

Hannah thumped him on the shoulder. He looked up and followed her pointing finger to a rusted van towing a utility trailer that bristled with lawn equipment. The van pulled into a service bay next to the groundskeeping building and stopped. Three men and a woman tumbled out of the van. They donned blotched straw Western hats as they scrambled to the trailer. Within seconds, small engines buzzed, and the workers owned the lawn.

Maytubby turned to Hannah and said, "I like the way groundskeeping maintains a remote facility for its equipment and employees."

"Nobody hobblin', either. Good foot care." Bond shifted into first and eased the Buick over faux cobblestone pavers. "Like the man said."

They slid back under the live oak canopy. Italianate and Spanish Colonial revival houses rose out of elaborate shrubbery and bright lily nooks. "Two-Twenty-One," Maytubby said.

Bond slowed as they approached the house. It was a Federal-style mansion—red brick, black shutters, and three dormers up in the sky. Security cameras perched like crows on the dormers. In the driveway, a light-blue Range Rover was parked beside a large white coupe.

Hannah downshifted to first. She and Maytubby pulled their caps down over their eyes. The Range Rover had a cardboard tag on which someone had inked "Stolen Tag" in Old English Gothic calligraphy. "Uptown tag," Maytubby said.

Bond squinted at the coupe. "You know what kind of car that is?"

Maytubby swiped off his mapping program and photographed the coupe's plate. "No. Drive around the block and I'll check under 'luxury coupes.'" Halfway around the block, he said, "Rolls-Royce Wraith, this year's."

"No wonder he treats his employees so good." Bond frowned as they made a second pass.

"Master of Bunion Manor," Maytubby said.

"Think he'll invite us over and grill some dove poppers?"

* * *

A few miles of affluent Dallas suburbia north, Longhorn Fly Fishing dominated a white stucco strip mall. SUVs rolled by on Lovers Lane as Maytubby and Bond threaded a maze of new Jeeps and Land Rovers in the store's parking lot. Maytubby had taken off his ball cap.

Inside, men and women with expensive haircuts were trying on waders and fishing vests, plucking flies from a display box, and wagging rods. Two thirtysomething men in pastel polo shirts leaned over a thin older man, watching him tie a fly.

Maytubby walked along a rack of fishing vests and stopped. He lifted one on a hanger and showed it to Bond. It was sewn in two shades of gray. "Look familiar?"

She nodded, then reached for the price tag and brought it to her face. She dropped it. "Dallas," she said.

The fly rods were arranged by length on a brightly lit slanted pine rack. Bond pointed to one of the nine-foot rods. "There," she said.

Maytubby picked it up by its cork handle and looked around for a free salesperson. He caught the eye of a weathered middle-aged man in khaki shorts and spanking-new trail boots with bright red stitching. The tanned man walked slowly toward Maytubby, but he was looking Bond over and shifting his lips a smidge.

Maytubby said, "My podiatrist, Dr. Archerd, tells me you guys have the best Woolly Buggers." Hannah looked at him. Maytubby jiggled the rod.

"Oh, I thought you were looking at the rod." The salesman's eyes darted to the fly case and back. Maytubby jiggled the rod some more.

The salesman pointed at the rod. "You know, Dr. Archerd was in here yesterday late. He bought one of those and some other equipment to replace tackle somebody stole out of his Range Rover up on the Blue

River in Oklahoma." The man put his hands on his hips and shook his head slowly.

"Oh, man," Maytubby said. A customer cranked an empty fly reel.

"I know." He leaned toward Maytubby and spoke softly, "Those Okies are a bunch of thievin' hillbillies."

Maytubby nodded once. "Damn straight. By cracky."

The salesman frowned and looked down, then up. "You want some Woolly Buggers?"

"One chartreuse, one gold." Maytubby followed him to the fly display box. "What's Dr. Archerd like?"

The clerk picked up a small cardboard box and a large pair of tweezers. He looked at Maytubby quizzically.

"Oh. I mean without the white coat. When he's not being a doctor."

The clerk tweezed out a chartreuse Woolly Bugger and dropped it in the box. He acted reflective.

After a few seconds, he shook his head and plucked out the gold fly. "Nah, man. I don't know any more than you do. Prob'ly less. He just took up fly fishing a month ago. Never came to a class." He slipped the gold fly into the box and closed it. As he walked to the register, he said, "Dr. Archerd had us rig up several flies to leaders and tie one of those leaders to his wet-tip fly line. He's a surgeon, so he must know all the knots. Maybe just one of those people who want servants. Ten-oh-five."

Maytubby handed him a ten and took a nickel from his pants pocket. Hannah stepped to the register.

The clerk handed Maytubby the box and a receipt. He looked out the front window and not at his customers when he said, "Tell you the truth? He didn't seem interested."

Maytubby took the box and reached for the clerk's hand. "Bill," he said.

The clerk took it and said, "Tyler."

Maytubby held up the box and shook it. "I'll let you know if these kill." The clerk nodded as Maytubby and Bond left the store.

"I heard that about him taking up fly fishing a month ago," Hannah said. "Uhhh. He bought stuff to replace what he says was stolen so it looks like the stuff was stolen." She unlocked the car doors and talked over the roof. "But he took up fly fishing just a month before his stuff was on the dead man. If he's part of this murder, that's ignorant."

* * *

Twenty minutes later, in Plano, Bond pulled off US 75 and parked the Skylark in front of a locked pipe gate blocking the Sitka Auto Ranch entrance. "Why is this closed on a Saturday?" she said.

"Blue law, like Oklahoma, but Texas says the business can close on either Saturday or Sunday."

An empty pickup was parked on the apron. A young couple strolled through the new-car lot. The shadows of mammoth American and Texas flags swam across the gleaming stock.

Maytubby and Bond, their caps pulled low, pretended to look at cars but worked their way steadily around the building. "You see security?" Bond said.

He nodded toward the parts entrance, then turned his head toward the cars. "Looks like two people, two vehicles. One man, one woman."

Hannah looked at them briefly. "That's a regular convention. Male in the white Crown Vic, female in the black whatever van."

When they had passed the vehicles, they continued straight down a row of pickups so they could return facing the building. Halfway back, Maytubby said, "Damn." Hannah turned abruptly away from him and walked fast toward the front of the building.

Maytubby caught up with her. "I know it was a coincidence, that Gautier's Transportation van, but . . ."

"You don't say the 'r' in that name?" she said.

"It's Cajun French. Why'd you run off?"

"That's not a woman in the van. That's Jimmy Nail, the hoser. In cahoots with Tiny, the Holy City guy. Didn't want him to see me lookin' at him in that van. When I'm on my hind feet, a Eighty-Niner hat idn't foolin' nobody."

When the building was between them and Nail, Maytubby walked to the showroom plate glass and slowed. Hannah walked behind him.

He stopped and pointed down at a sales literature table. "There."

She looked at a shiny flyer for Gautier Medical Transportation. In the header photo, a polished black Nissan Taxi with the Gautier logo was parked on a pastoral road. Groomed sorrel quarter horses grazed in a rolling pasture behind it. Bullet points listed testimonials. "They treated my mother like their own mother." In a second photo, a medevac helicopter rose in the sky over a Gautier van.

"Got a city printer. But a slick tract can spell rough business."

"Don't turn around, Hannah. Look at the reflection, toward the entrance."

The Gautier van idled inside the pipe gate, the driver's door open. Jimmy Nail unlocked a padlock and swung the gate open. He drove through the gate, got out, and locked it behind him. As he walked back to the van, he turned toward the rear of the Skylark and stopped. Then he got back in the van and turned north on US 75.

Maytubby said, "He know your car?"

"He's only seen it at night. For less than a minute."

"You know how far back we'll have to stay in the tail."

Now they were jogging toward the gate. "'Bout six miles," Hannah said.

* * *

The Taxi made its first turn in Sherman. Nail took Peyton Drive to the post office. He circled through its parking lot, gusts of smoke coming from the driver's window, and drove right past Maytubby and Bond on his way back to US 75. He didn't seem to notice, so Bond made a U-turn and followed him. "The 'may be found at' address is right there on Peyton, almost next door." She pointed over her shoulder. "Looks like an abandoned tool shed."

When Nail was well on his way back to Plano, Bond looked at Maytubby and said, "Enough?"

"Yeah."

She turned the Skylark around and drove toward the Red River. "No passenger, no doctors," she said. "He went to one of our PO's."

"Maybe it was a practice run."

"Yeah," Hannah said. "I wonder how many groundskeepers live in the Sherman post office."

"He's washing money," Maytubby said.

"Takin' his odometer home from the doctor's," Hannah said.

Hannah turned on her headlights when they crossed the Red River. She said, "My foot feels funny."

Maytubby grinned. "Come to think of it, I'm getting a sore toe."

CHAPTER 15

Maytubby's phone woke him at 3:21 a.m. Faint moonlight laddered through his Venetian blinds. The name on the screen was Deb Laber. He accepted the call, said "Maytubby," and sat on the side of the bed, reaching for his jeans with his right hand.

"Sergeant."

"Yes, Ms. Laber. Are you and Jason together inside your house?" Maytubby pulled up his jeans.

"Yes. Could you come here?" He put on a black jacket, switching his phone ear and shoulder. "On my way. Tell me."

"Somebody called my landline and then hung up. I don't have a yard light. I think maybe they were trying to get me to turn on a light in the house so they could see the house from the road. I can hear a vehicle going back and forth up there. Maybe a truck. No lights. My house lights were just on a second or two."

He slipped on his worn New Balance trail runners and slung his duty belt over his head. "The vehicle loud, like a bad muffler?"

"No."

"Not Raleigh Creech, then." Maytubby thumped across his long porch, under the single dangling light bulb. "Jason's father knows where your house is?"

The old Ford pickup gushed to life. "I'm on the road, Ms. Laber. Keep talking."

"His dad knows where we live. He doesn't need a light."

"So not him," Maytubby said, rolling through a red light on Mississippi Street.

"Not him." Maytubby heard her breathing. "We have a loaded four-ten single-shot."

"Any time you feel you're in danger, I can call the Highway Patrol and the Johnston County Sheriff, but I'm probably going to get there sooner."

"Okay."

"Jason has stayed inside at night?"

"Far as I know."

"I'm going to hang up, notify the Lighthorse Police, and drive. Call back if you need to." Maytubby briefly told the night dispatcher he was en route in his own pickup, then slid the phone in his jacket pocket. US 377 ran straight south through the old oil mecca Fittstown. Between Pontotoc and Connerville, the flash of a deer's eye made him hit his brakes. The Ford idled while three does cantered across the asphalt and bounded over a cattle fence. Before Maytubby could release the clutch, two coyotes loped across the road toward them.

As he neared Pennington Creek, dolomite boulders loomed up from the prairie. His phone came to life. "Ms. Laber. Three minutes."

She whispered now. "Good. The motor sound stopped, and a door slammed a little south on the road. I wish I had a mean dog."

"I'll stay on the line until I get to the gate." Maytubby crossed Pennington Creek and turned south.

"I have all the shades up so we can see out. The moon is poor help."

His headlights threw shadows behind prickly pear and yucca. A half mile before the Labers' ranch gate, he shut them off. Then he silenced his cell phone. Closer in, he switched the engine off, coasting downhill in neutral until he reached the ranch gate. He did not see a parked vehicle. At the gate, he parked the Ford and buckled on his duty belt. He had disabled the cab light years ago.

Three strides, and Maytubby scissor-vaulted the fence, holding the top of a cedar post. He hit the driveway in a sprint, kept to the quiet sandy ruts. Four-tenths of a mile, he had told Hannah. Four minutes and change. Somebody parked farther down Bellwood Road would have more space to cover but might have set out sooner.

Moonlight glowed dully on the ruts, guiding Maytubby to the little house. Soon, over his footfalls he could hear Pennington Creek rippling. Far to the east, a chuck-will's-widow piped its name.

Just as the metal roof of the Laber house came into view, a flash lit its windows, followed instantly by the thick report of a shotgun. There was brief silence, then a rhythmic, mechanical pounding. Now Maytubby could make out a tall figure at the front door, torso angled back for the kicks.

The man turned his head toward Maytubby a second before Maytubby took out his support leg with a cut block. A word caught in the man's throat as he fell.

As Maytubby scrambled to his feet, the man rolled to his hands and knees in a sprinter's crouch, ducked his head, and took off down the drive. His stride was stiff but effective—that of an older person in shape. He veered off the drive and vanished into the alders along the creek.

Maytubby called through the door, "It's Sergeant Maytubby. He's gone."

A dead bolt ticked, and the door opened a couple of inches. Maytubby couldn't see inside. The door opened all the way. He smelled gunpowder. "Are you both okay?" he said softly. "I heard a gunshot."

"We're okay," Deborah Laber said. "Jason fired a warning shot. Into our ceiling. He felt the kicks."

"I have to stand outside and listen. I didn't see a vehicle on the road. I'll stay here in case there's someone else."

"I think it's south of the drive, around the bend."

Maytubby took a few steps away from the house and stood still. In a few seconds, Deborah and Jason stepped out the door and stood still. Jason's break-action .410 was open, tented over his left forearm. Maytubby heard him bite his nails.

The moon had almost set. The fleeing man's thrashing faded to silence. Some coyotes keened in the distance. A freight blew for the Main Street crossing in Mill Creek, miles to the west.

About three minutes passed before an engine came to life. The attacker knew his way through those woods. Even if the same guy lugged the body to Pennington Creek, he might not have seen the house from there.

The muscular engine reminded Maytubby of the Ford's carbureted V-8, which was as big as a washing machine.

Maytubby looked at the Labers in the indigo light. They were looking at him. The engine noise Dopplered up. It was coming north, toward Maytubby's pickup. Deb Laber turned her head toward Bellwood Road. A penumbra crept above the headlights. An early rooster crowed far away.

The vehicle stopped and idled near where the Ford was parked. Two doors must have opened, up there, because Maytubby heard two slams. After the second, the vehicle roared away. Maytubby thought of the spare ignition key taped to the Ford's steering column. The one he left in the lock cylinder would be deep in the weeds.

"Do you have a Sunday shift at Sipokni?" Maytubby said.

"No." Deb Laber brushed her son's shoulders and tousled his hair. "My ears are ringing."

"I'll sit out here the rest of the night."

She blew air through her lips. Resignation, Maytubby thought.

"Do you have anyone you could stay with until we settle these thugs?"

"These?" she said.

"It looks like more than one person is involved in the murder."

She sighed. "That's special."

Maytubby was quiet for a minute.

"Mostly Jason's dad's folks around here. No room at the inn, if you know what I mean. Bad blood." She put her arm around her son. "I haven't had a cigarette since this one was born. Tonight, I woulda backslid."

From down on the quarry spur came the distant thunder of coupling sand cars.

“Deputy Hannah Bond lives in north Tish,” Maytubby said. “It’s close. Let me ask her if you and Jason could crash there a few days.”

“The tall cop?”

“Yeah.”

“She doesn’t seem very, uh . . .”

“Touchy-feely?”

Deb Laber folded her arms and chafed her biceps. “No—I mean, yes.”

Jason leaned away from his mother and kicked the ground. He stopped and yawned loudly.

“Hannah grew up rough. She—”

“So did I,” Deb Laber said. “I’m trying to make sure Jason doesn’t.” She extended one hand and opened it toward the creek. “And here we are.”

“Not your fault.”

“Mmm. I’m tired. You say the deputy is okay?”

“Yes.”

Jake brakes hissed on State 1. A vehicle passed on Bellwood Road, going pretty fast.

“I’ll sleep on it. If I can sleep.” She gently pushed her son, and they walked to the door. After he had gone inside, she turned to Maytubby and said, “If we come, we’re bringing the gun.”

* * *

A faint gold backlit the sycamores. There was a distant chorus of roosters. Maytubby could see his breath. He pulled his jacket tighter as he followed the intruder’s path toward the alders. Just beyond the driveway, he took out his phone and clicked on its flash. Most of the prints in the sand were blurred by gravel or speed. Almost to the first saplings, he found two prints that were intact—a left and a right. The tread matched his own trail runners, right down to the long diamond cut in the heel. He pulled off a shoe and set it beside the print before photographing them. His shoe looked like a child’s.

At 6:45, he phoned Hannah, who was walking to the Johnston County Courthouse for a Sunday shift. She carried a long-handled three-tine cultivator older than she was. She switched phone and tool hands and said, "You already had your prunes and mush?"

"I wish."

"Lard biscuits and fried chicken gizzards, I'm tellin' you."

"You almost snared me with Louisiana tasso once," Maytubby said.

Hannah laughed. "Then it got eat by a dog. You stayed pure."

An owl sailed over Pennington Creek. "Hannah, I'm at the Laber house. A man tried to break in last night. Deb Laber heard a vehicle on Bellwood Road and called me. I ran him off before he could get inside."

"Too dark to see his face?"

"Yeah, he was spry but maybe a little older. Tall. Seemed to know the woods but not where the house is. Somebody called her, she thinks to make her turn on her light. Probably him. Her ex knows where the house is, so not him. The vehicle wasn't noisy enough to be Creech's.

"You hear it after the guy left?" Hannah said.

"Sounded like an old truck with a big eight."

"You sure he didn't steal your Ford?"

Maytubby said, "He could have. I think he just stopped and threw my key in the weeds."

"Doesn't know you very well." Maytubby heard traffic passing Bond. She said, "Damn! Magaw's civvie car and an OSBI Charger at the courthouse before seven on a Sunday morning. Must be the end-times." She breathed into the phone. Gravel crunched. "Okay, Bill. You could've told me all this at a decent hour. Laber works at that Old West place, and the deaf kid goes to Sulphur. Closer to me than you."

Maytubby watched the brightening sky while Bond leaned the cultivator against her cruiser and got buzzed into the sheriff's office. She said, "Mom on the couch, kid on the floor. You know where I keep the spare key."

"Deb Laber said she's not going anywhere without her four-ten."

"Somebody gets shot on my porch, you never told me that." She ended the call.

In the gathering light, Maytubby followed the Labers' drive to Bellwood Road and let himself out the gap gate. He stopped behind the Ford's tailgate on the driver's side. Trail runner prints like those in the driveway led to and from his truck's open window. He photographed them. The key he had left in the ignition was gone, but he could see his spare down on the column. The key-chucker could have reached it without laying a hand on the truck. The 20-gauge pump Maytubby racked on the cab ceiling was still there. Tire prints from passing vehicles had erased some of the shoe prints. The door kicker had parked behind the pickup, half in the bar ditch. Considerate of other motorists, or writing down Maytubby's plate? Some of the tire prints that erased the shoe prints belonged to the intruder.

Maytubby found the spot where the shoe prints exited from and reentered the vehicle. Then he laid his driver's license beside the tire prints of the intruder's vehicle, for scale, and photographed them. Wheels could be swapped on old vehicles, so the prints might tell him nothing.

He untaped the spare pickup key from the steering column, rolled up the driver's window, locked the truck, and pocketed the key.

As he walked back down the drive, he smelled coffee. When he entered the Labers' yard, Deb was standing on the porch, in a T-shirt and jeans, frowning into an old jadeite glass mug. She looked up and half smiled. "I thought you were standing guard."

"Nature called."

She nodded. "Men always like a country leak. You want some coffee?"

"Sure," he said.

The instant she turned into the house, Maytubby scooted to the alders and relieved himself.

He was back in place when she returned. He took the mug she offered him, and blew gently to cool the coffee. They stood in silence for some minutes, looking into the woods. It was full daylight now, though they stood in the shadows of the tall sycamores.

Maytubby said, "I spoke with Deputy Bond an hour ago. She has invited you and Jason to stay with her in Tish until all this blows over."

Deb Laber frowned and nodded as she drank from the mug. "*Chokma*," she said. "*Yakoke*. Thank you. That's about all I know."

Maytubby shrugged, "Me, too, more or less." He paused. "Deputy

Bond studies the language in night class. She probably knows more than both of us."

Deb Laber chortled. "Okay. Let me roust Jason. I'll fry some eggs. Then we'll pack up and follow you into Tish."

Maytubby nodded. Then he touched his cheek with two fingers. "Do me a favor and ask him if all his traps are tripped and empty. If he doesn't know, I'll come back with him and run them. No reason any critters should suffer."

"Sure," she said.

CHAPTER 16

"Morning, Hannah." Sheriff Magaw held out a Styrofoam cup of black coffee. He wore a civilian suit and tie that Hannah recognized as his church clothes. She took the coffee and slid her time card from the wall holder. She gestured toward his outfit with her coffee cup. "Sunrise service?" She clocked in and replaced the card in its slot.

"Easter's next week, Deputy."

She shrugged.

Magaw cocked his head, and she followed him down the hall. When he turned into an empty interrogation room, she could see Agent Scrooby farther down the hall. He was holding a coffee cup and talking on his cell phone. He looked at the floor.

After Magaw closed the door, Hannah said, "Dan Scrooby in Tish at seven on Sunday morning?"

Magaw frowned. Though the door was shut, he spoke softly. "ME and OSBI forensics made a preliminary finding."

"Burnin' the midnight oil," she said.

"Douglas Verner was brained with rebar a good while before his body made it to Pennington Creek. One blow. The laceration showed the rebar pattern."

"The stuff on the rock?"

"Probably catfish bloodbait."

"*Pfffttt*," she said.

Magaw raised his eyebrows and sipped his coffee. "Still, lot of bait stands around Lake Texoma."

Bond rubbed her chin. "So what tore Scrooby away from his Sunday breakfast? I doubt he drove all the way to Tish to call on bait houses."

Magaw stared past her shoulder. "He and I woke up Curt Fenton and brought him in for questioning." Now he looked at Bond again. "Agent Scrooby says you made friends with Curt at a domestic." He smiled faintly.

Hannah said nothing.

"Looked like he was sleeping on the couch this morning." Magaw grinned.

Bond drank some coffee and set her cup on the table. "What about Tula Verner, who fixed her husband's wagon?"

Magaw wiped the grin off his face and nodded. "She's back here, too. Her lawyer . . ."

"Possum face."

"Yeah. On his way up from Texas. Tula's already smashed." He took a step toward the door. "Deputy, Scrooby said to tell you thanks for pointing out Curt Fenton's big feet . . ."

"And to tell me to butt out."

"Yeah," Magaw said, nodding. "I need you to go out and catch some speeders on Highway Seven by Wapanucka."

* * *

The possum-faced lawyer drove into the courthouse parking lot just as Bond was ducking into her cruiser. She watched him firm the knot on his red tie, open the trunk of his yellow Porsche Boxster, and pull out the metal briefcase. After he had gone inside, Bond drove behind his car and took out her phone. The dealer decal and plate frame were both from Sitka Auto Ranch in Plano. She photographed the plate.

On her way out of town, Bond stopped on the shoulder of Main at Sooner Foods. The man on the lawn tractor was still at it, mowing the lawn he had already mowed. Bond looked toward the Fenton house.

There were two cars in the driveway and one in the alley. The one in the alley was a Charger. Bond recognized the man leaning against it as the rookie, Cable. She made a U-turn on Main, drove back to US 377, and headed north.

There were faint wisps of green in the oak savannah, the rising sun kindling redbuds in the understory. Buzzard Creek swerved out of the Big Rock and into a riprap channel underneath the highway.

As she approached the Blue River on Oklahoma 7, she slowed and eased off the shoulder, into a stand of sumac at the foot of a massive sycamore. The sumac hid her from traffic, and she could watch the stream froth against cedar snags. She turned on her radar and watched the numbers as pickups and stock trucks shushed by.

Just off the highway, the two small parking lots for the public fishing area were empty. Trout season was over. Bond wondered whether the foot doctor had parked in one of these, on the north boundary of public land, or in one of those at the opposite end, two miles south, when his fancy gear got kiped. *If* it was kiped. If he was even here.

The waders on the body went up to his chest. The vest was over that. Anybody wearing those, it would make sense to wait until he got off the river and back to his vehicle and pull them all off so he could pee. He would have worn jeans underneath the waders. Bond looked at the two tiny lots. Each would fit ten vehicles, tops. That foot doctor was likely a priss, but how far would he walk to hide himself from almost nobody? And if he walked toward where she was parked, he would see anybody coming to or from the lot. He would have to walk pretty far the other way to get to a place where he couldn't see the lot.

Bond gently tom-tommed the heel of her hand on the steering wheel while she watched a sharp-shinned hawk plucking its songbird breakfast on a stump. Then she held her hand still for a beat before she slammed it against the wheel. "Bullshit!" she said aloud. The only reason Archerd would have come here was so he could be a lookout while his pals removed his gear and Texas tags, and then wait for a fisherman to come along and see him peeing. Somebody would have seen him fishing in his waders, and somebody would have seen him peeing. But why . . .

Bond's cell phone buzzed in her front pants pocket. The number was not in her contacts, but it was the local 580 area code.

"Johnston County Deputy Hannah Bond," she said.

There was hoarse coughing, then throat-clearing. "Deputy . . ." The whisper faded.

"That's right. How can I help you?"

"This is Maxine Fenton. You, uh—"

"I know who you are," Bond said.

"My . . . my . . ." Her voice wavered. Then it found force. "Doug Verner has been killed!"

Bond spotted an oncoming livestock semi. She checked her radar. It flashed 88. She scowled and turned off the device. The truck's brakes squealed as it passed.

"Yeah," Bond said. She waited to see if Maxine would tell her something she didn't know.

"He's dead!"

Bond waited while Maxine Fenton wept. A Lexus sedan shot by the sumac stand, doing at least a hundred. Bond looked at her dark radar screen and scowled again.

"Deputy?"

"Here."

"Remember I told you I was seeing someone?" Maxine said.

"Yeah."

"It was Doug Verner," she whispered.

Bond rolled her eyes and said nothing.

"He was so lonely. His horrible drunken wife, running with scum. Scum!"

Bond heard Maxine breathing thickly.

"Some officers were just here. They woke up my husband and me and said they were taking him to the county jail for questioning in Doug's murder. He turned white and puked again—on the living room floor—before they dragged him out. Deputy, Curt just got in from Nocona, Texas, yesterday morning. Right before the neighbors complained and you came in. He said he had driven half the night after somebody called his cell to snitch on Doug and me. How they got his cell I don't know. He went to the Nod Inn, where Doug and I got together." Maxine's voice had lost its waver.

Bond watched scofflaws roar past her window—hundreds of speeding-fine dollars vanishing from her quota. The call was thieving her time for searching the trails.

"Curt can be gone for weeks. He sells hardware to small stores up and down the plains. You saw him, Deputy Bond. I know he was rattled then. But he is normally a bland man, a backslapper. Afraid of what people think. I've never seen an ounce of fight in him. He's even, uh, shy in bed. He would never *kill* someone." Bond heard a mechanical noise in the background. Maybe a dishwasher. "Somebody got in our tool shed—"

Bond interrupted her. "You said 'scum,' ma'am."

"What?"

"That Douglas Verner's wife was running with scum."

"Oh. Oh, God, he was afraid of them."

Bond heard some scuffing in the background. She heard Maxine say, "Who are you, Officer?" She couldn't make out the response, only some mumbling. Then she heard Maxine say, "I'm talking to my sister." Two seconds later, Maxine said, "G'bye, sis." And hung up.

Bond looked at her phone and said, "Good work, rookie." She turned on her radar and watched a rafter of turkeys amble into the woods.

* * *

Agent Cable did not ruin the hunt after all. Palm Sunday gave people the lead foot. In two hours, she stopped six speeders, two of them for twenty over. One of those was the Lexus sedan.

Hannah checked her watch. Sheriff Magaw wouldn't have worn his Sunday clothes if he weren't going to church after the interrogation. He would be in his Tishomingo First Baptist pew for another half hour.

She drove off the highway shoulder and into the empty lot on the south side of the road, parked, and took the cultivator from the trunk. First, she walked every inch of the dirt lot, seining up candy wrappers, dislodging beer cans, snagging nests of monofilament. Then she shouldered the tool and walked through a pedestrian gate between the fence and a steel vehicle gate. She stood in the middle of an old jeep trail. The trail paralleled the Blue River for a third of a mile before it played out among stony shelves above the stream. Faint paths split left from the trail and crossed rocky meadows of feathery little bluestem, on their way to angling perches. The low roar of a falls muffled the highway traffic.

Why would Archerd involve himself in a crime so close to his own interests? Better camouflage?

Or even if the killer was in cahoots with Archerd, the foot doctor may have had nothing to do with the murder. The killer might have known where he was and stolen his new gear and tags to stage Pennington Creek, improvising in an emergency.

Bond walked five hundred yards on the jeep trail, then took two steps to the left on a fainter track. She lowered the cultivator, pulled back a knot of grass, looked at the space, swung the tines a bit to the left, and repeated. Then, after completing the arc, she stepped backward toward the lot and began a new arc in the opposite direction.

The work was slow and dull. Almost an hour passed before she came to the lot fence.

She had found a few empty cans of cheap beer but mostly light packaging for fishing tackle—hook cards, split-shot wrappers, marshmallow bags—that wind had blown from the riverbank. If the pissing doctor had pulled out a cell phone, whatever was in his phone pocket would get dropped first. Tackle would have stayed with his vest, which had to come off before the waders.

Her shoulder radio had been quiet. Magaw and his wife would be dipping catfish nuggets in tartar sauce at Fish Tales. Bond would lay good money Agent Scrooby was there, too, excavating the buffet. As she would have done.

She stepped a few yards to her left, turned south, and put the cultivator to work again. This time, Bond walked forward, paralleling the route she had just finished. The midday sun made her break a sweat. Her strokes with the cultivator brought back much hotter days in her ninth and tenth summers, when one of her foster fathers made her hoe cotton from sunup to sundown. This was a walk in the park.

The end of her circuit brought her near the river woods. Bond shouldered the cultivator and walked into the shade of post oaks. A gap of more than two hours in her citations was going to stick out. She took off her hat, wiped her face with her forearm.

She heard a vehicle decelerate on the highway.

Glancing at the ground before she took her first step toward the cruiser, Bond saw, among the deer pellets and acorn caps, a little curl of pear-colored paper. She took vinyl gloves from her duty belt and snapped them on. Then she knelt on the ground, picked up the paper by its corner, and shook dirt off it.

A flash made her look up. A large new black pickup had parked between her and the cruiser. A tall man wearing an orange ball cap and a blue jacket scooted out of the truck, walked behind it, and stood behind the cruiser. He then walked to the vehicle gate and leaned against the cross pipe, facing her way. Bond couldn't tell whether he was old or young. She saw no Mosaic gray hair. A cap and jacket could hide that. She wished for her Steiners, on the cruiser's passenger floor.

When the pickup was well on its way to Wapanucka, Bond stood and held up the strip of paper. It was a gas receipt from a Quik Trip in Plano, dated Thursday. The last day of trout season. She held it to her nose. It smelled only of cedar needles. She tipped it into a plastic evidence bag and stowed the bag in her belt. Then she stuck an evidence marker at the base of the oak and photographed it in context. Lots of north Texans on the Blue when the season opened in November. Fewer fishermen—and more of them Okies—toward the end of the season.

Back in her sumac blind, Hannah wondered how Palm Sunday had put ants in the pants of Johnston County's drivers. They filled her daily quota, which Sheriff Magaw called her "productivity goal," before 5 p.m., when she reached for her sack lunch: two fried-bologna sandwiches with Jack cheese and jalapeños. Neither Tiny's old Dodge nor the new black pickup disturbed her peace.

CHAPTER 17

A Sooner Foods bag hung from Maytubby's left hand while he held Bond's screen door open with his right elbow. Deb and Jason Laber stood behind him, watched him turn the dented knob and open her front door.

Deb laid her palm on the screen frame and let her son pass into the house behind Maytubby. Then she eased it shut. Maytubby noted this.

"The deputy doesn't lock her door?" Deb said.

Maytubby set the bag on the kitchen table and pulled out an apple and a box of raisins he had bought for himself. The room smelled of fried meat and gun oil. He looked at the door. "No. We have an old joke about where she hides the secret key."

Deb Laber scratched her temple with an index finger. She was vexed.

"There's not even a real key to that door. I guess you could lean one of these chairs under the inside knob."

She shook her head, glum.

"Let's go bring in your stuff." Maytubby tried to sound upbeat.

The Labers' sunburned Neon was parked in a nest of spirea shrubs, hidden from US 377 by Hannah's house. Maytubby had guided her in. Now Deb opened the trunk and handed Jason two backpacks and two pillows. He waited a few seconds and then made way for Maytubby. Deb handed him an old hard-shell suitcase and a sleeping bag. She brought out the shotgun, her palm under its broken breech to show that it was unloaded.

As they walked back to the house, Maytubby said to Deb, "Detective Bond—you should call her Hannah. She said you should take the couch, and Jason the living room floor. Hannah's not fussy." He opened the screen for them. "But those rib eyes in the bag? For hers, the rarer the better. She's off at seven." He handed Deb one of Bond's cards. "Her cell number is handwritten."

Deb and Jason laid their things on the floor at one end of the couch and stood in the middle of the dining-living room. They looked at the bare walls, the lumpy couch and scuffed Formica table. Deb suddenly cut Maytubby a glance, her face shedding its sadness. "Thanks for finding us a place," she said. Jason watched her lips. She started signing. "We'll make Hannah a nice supper. We're not persnickety, either."

"You're welcome." Now Jason was watching Maytubby's mouth. "There's a sign for 'persnickety'?"

She smiled sadly and repeated it, thumbs under index fingers, the index fingernails pecking each other like birds. "Finicky," she said.

Jason barked out a laugh. He brought his hands very near his face, squinted, and repeated the sign in miniature, satirizing fussiness.

* * *

Maytubby parked next to the Chickasaw Council House Museum, a stately granite Gothic overlooking Tishomingo. He called the manager of Heartland Aviation at Ada Municipal Airport.

"Hey, Frank. Bill Maytubby."

"Hey, Bill. You renting the Learjet Seventy-Five, same as usual?" Country music played in the background.

"Maybe. Is that tail number two niner foxtrot?"

"Uh, no, Bill. Two nine foxtrot is a 1959 Cessna One-Fifty."

"Oh, right," Maytubby said.

"Save you six thousand an hour."

"You're always looking out for me, Frank."

* * *

Forty-five minutes later, Maytubby stood in a spanking-new Ada terminal, funded in part by the Chickasaw Nation. Soft polarized light from floor-to-ceiling windows fell on steel-blue upholstery and carpet. The room smelled like fabric sizing. Not a single person was in the building.

The Heritage Aviation office was in an adjacent hangar. Frank held out the 150's key. "Why don't you fly some of the nation's equipment?"

Maytubby took the key and shrugged. "Technically, I'm off duty."

Frank nodded.

"But really?" Maytubby canted his head. "If I pay for the plane, I own what I do in it."

"Yeah," Frank said, "like you spook a prize stallion and the rancher sues you and not the nation."

"Exactly, Frank. Thanks for the hypothetical."

Frank threw an elbow and made a clicking sound to show he was joshing.

When Maytubby had finished his preflight checks, he cracked the cabin door and shouted, "Clear!" though not a soul was anywhere near the propeller. He shut the door and set the altimeter at 1,016 feet—the airport's elevation. He snugged the paper sack with his field glasses and snacks against the passenger seat back.

On the apron of runway 35, he braked to a stop, then gently pushed in the throttle knob as he braked the left wheel and slowly spun the plane around so he could look for air traffic in every direction.

There was no tower, so Maytubby radioed Ada UNICOM to signal his intentions. He taxied onto the runway and plunged the throttle to the dash. The old Continental engine did its work, and the Cessna was soon aloft, vaning slightly eastward. Downtown Ada, then King's Road mansions, slid under the landing gear as he flew south.

When he could see the Laber house on his left, he banked toward it. Then he leveled off, cut the RPMs, and added one click of flaps to slow his speed. He was looking for collections of junk vehicles that might once have included the Hudson. The forest canopy had not fully leafed out, which was a help. He couldn't say the same about the grass: a little later in the spring, he could have spotted a rectangle of dead grass cut out of a green pasture.

Johnston County was ranch country. Equipment junk heaps there were smaller than those on big farms, but there were still rusted tedders and balers, tractors, and mowing machines. And, of course, pickups and larger flatbed hay trucks.

Maytubby wove in shallow banks north and south, following Highway 7 toward the Blue River. When he saw a patch of junk, he picked up his field glasses for a closer look. Many of the vehicles were already retired when the Hudson was new—at work when FDR was president. Before Deb's restaurant came into view, he had already seen a junkyard buckboard.

The teal-blue ponds of the Tishomingo National Fish Hatchery crept under the Cessna's tires.

White cattle egrets rode Herefords and black Angus grazing in the swales. A few pump jacks worked on neat graveled production pads. He saw a pen of goats and a sounder of wild hogs.

Crossing US 377, he spotted a promising junkyard a half mile north of the highway. He banked left and circled the yard, glassing its perimeter. Vines and weeds had overgrown the place, and nothing had disturbed the ground around it for a long time.

The small parking lot for anglers on the Blue had emptied after trout season. When he was almost directly over the lots, he saw two vehicles on the Highway 7 south lot. One was law. When he got closer, he saw Hannah's number on the roof. The other was a new black pickup. Somebody was standing behind Hannah's cruiser. Whoever it was wore an orange cap and a blue jacket. Maytubby did a turn around that point until Orange Cap got in the pickup. As the Cessna banked out of the circle toward Bromide, Maytubby smiled to himself. Hannah had been writing tickets on 7 so she could moonlight on their case.

Just as the limestone ruins of Bromide's faded bathhouses nosed under his left wing, he looked straight down on the wild cursive of Delaware Creek. Butcher Pen Road ran alongside the creek. Maytubby cut the throttle even more and lowered the plane's nose in a gentle descent, banking into a wide spiral so he could get closer to the land.

Going west, he soon found the old quarry Hannah had mentioned.

And there in its shallow pit were the square buildings she said were meant to recreate the Holy City of the Wichitas. A figure stood beside an old truck, looking up at the Cessna. Another pickup was leaving the quarry in the direction of Butcher Pen Road. Also older, judging by its short bed and running boards. Aqua, like the '57 Chevy belonging to Steel-Toe at Foot Kingdom. Maytubby saw no junkyard in Old Jerusalem, so he cruised west. Within thirty seconds, he saw a rusted metal roof, notched by three chimneys. A territorial house.

Then he saw, just beyond it, a sight to make Raleigh Creech squirm with envy: a two-acre junkyard. A little right rudder brought him right over it. Machines from many decades, rusted by Gulf moisture. At one corner, he saw a knot of fresh ruts. A thin tangle of them led away from the junk toward the east. Maytubby turned the plane to follow the trail. He glassed the pastures and saw that the trail crossed a fence line and led through the holy quarry and onto Butcher Pen Road.

Suddenly, there came a light clattering on the fuselage, like tiny hail. A second later, he heard a faint *thump* through his closed windows. He trained his binoculars on the old truck. "Damn!' he said, shoving the throttle full in and banking in a steep climb away from the quarry. The figure beside the truck was holding a long gun. So not hail but birdshot. At this altitude, buckshot might have done some mischief. A .243 slug from a deer rifle might have turned him and the plane into a dark smudge on the Delaware bottom. He would ask Hannah more about her friend Tiny.

As the Cessna climbed, Maytubby saw the dust cloud of the aqua pickup just ahead of him. Since the truck had been parked in the quarry, he indulged his curiosity. A slight headwind meant he could stay behind the truck without circling back.

Butcher Pen Road T-boned a state highway. The aqua truck turned north and sped through the Amish hamlet of Clarita, slaloming around black one-horse carriages. At the intersection of State 31, the pickup turned right. It crossed the Choctaw national border and the Clear Boggy, then entered Coalgate, an old mining town where Trooper Renaldo's Italian forebear once worked a mine called Pinch Along. Downtown, the truck turned south on Broadway, drove a few blocks, and turned into the driveway of a house once rented by the late Wiley Bates, a meth mule who was incinerated by some of his confederates. The house was across the street from the South Liquor Store. The store's owner, Lorenza Mercante, had kept an eye on Bates for Maytubby.

It was Sunday; the store would be closed. But he saw a car parked in the rear. The Coalgate airport, a small hangar and a grass strip, was just behind the liquor store. Maytubby descended, turned into the traffic pattern, half-circled the field, and landed into the north breeze.

CHAPTER 18

As he taxied back toward the store, he folded his field glasses and stowed them in his back pocket. He parked on a grass apron well off the runway. Before leaving the plane, he briefly checked the prop for nicks, looked under the wings and fuselage, and found no paint damage from the birdshot.

Lorenza Mercante's back was turned toward the store's rear window when Maytubby stood on the back step. She was beheading a case of Heaven Hill vodka with an orange box cutter. Her important chestnut hair swept her shoulders. Maytubby waited until she had retracted the knife before he knocked on the window.

She spun around wide-eyed and stared at him for three seconds, grinned, and hurried to unlock the door. She said, "This is the second time you've come to visit without your clothes." She motioned him in, continued to beckon and nod as she said, "I mean . . ."

"My policeman suit," he said.

She choked on a laugh. "Yuh . . . yeah." She pretended to steady herself by grasping his forearm. "Muff, muffet—what was that word for regular clothes you said was Chickasaw but wasn't."

"Oh. Mufti." He smiled and looked at her hand.

She left it there a second longer before turning and craning her head to look out the front window. "Where's your police car?" She faced him again and blinked. "Wait. I remember I called you and snitched on Wiley Bates when you were flying. Chasing somebody. I said you should fly down here someday. And you did." She ran her fingers through her hair and leaned against the checkout counter. "On a Sunday." She arched her brows.

Maytubby was not so good that he wanted the moment to end. He laid his hand on an unopened case of Mogen David 20/20 Electric Melon and smiled until he felt weird. Then he said, "I need your help again, Miz—"

"Ut!" she made the "Halt!" sign and frowned a little.

"Lorenza," he said.

"Yes," she said. She rattled the box knife in her left hand. "But I wish it was pleasure."

"That, too. It's good to see you." Her eyes felt a little hot, so he looked down at the Mad Dog box.

She followed his glance and took a quick step toward him. "*Porca puttana!*" She used her Italian miner ancestors' word. "You would pick that box."

"I didn't notice."

She grasped his wrist, led him to the next box—a case of Zinfandel—and set his hand down on it. She patted his hand and gave him a more muted smile.

"And if I had," he said, "I wouldn't have doubted your taste."

Lorenza Mercante turned and looked out the front window toward a beat frame house across Broadway. Maytubby did the same. She said, "It's about that house where Wiley lived, isn't it?"

"Yeah," Maytubby said quietly.

"Maybe somebody should look into that landlord."

"Have . . ."

"That aqua Chevy pickup?" she pointed through the plate glass. "Coming and going the last month. Tall dude, middle-aged, short hair. Never spends the night that I can tell. Doesn't buy booze here. At least Wiley was good for his daily Heaven Hill Old Style." She laid the box cutter on the counter, walked around the Zin case on the stock table, and stood beside Maytubby.

She leaned until she just touched him. She smelled like lavender and cardboard. Her detective work made her feel closer, Maytubby guessed.

She said, "A couple times, there's been another vehicle there, a black van with white lettering. I can't tell the makes of those vans apart."

"Lemme get my phone." Maytubby gently nudged her as he reached into his left pants pocket. She didn't move but let his elbow trace her ribs. He scrolled through his photos until he found the Nissan Taxi passenger van with "Gautier's Transportation" on the side.

"Like this?"

Before he could raise the phone to her, she bent to look at the screen, her hair brushing his chin. When she straightened, her face was closer. He felt her breath.

"Probably. It's hard to see when you're so far away."

"Right," he said.

She looked into his eyes and squinted. "Don't you think?"

Maytubby felt his hands go clammy. Double entendre was his fiancée's prerogative. He didn't break eye contact—it felt good—but he stepped back and put his phone away, then pulled his small field glasses from his hip pocket.

She looked at the binoculars, frowned, and nodded. "Welcome to Lorenza's deer blind," she said, opening her palm toward the front window. "Knock yourself out." She picked up her box cutter, held it in front of her face, snarled, and play-feinted when she ran out the blade. Maytubby laughed.

When she went to work on another box, Maytubby stood in a little recess and watched the house and truck. "I saw that old Chevy in Dallas," he said. "I could kick myself for not snapping its tag."

"Look here," she said, again laying her knife on the table. She rushed out the back door. Through a window, Maytubby saw her get in her car. The car reappeared out the front window. It exited from the gravel lot, crossed Broadway, and stopped behind the old Chevy. The brake lights dimmed, and the car made a left at the next intersection. Seconds later, it reentered the parking lot.

When Lorenza Mercante burst in the back door, she recited the Texas plate: three letters and four numbers. "Thank—"

"Quick!" She pointed to the front window. Maytubby spun around and raised his binoculars. Just as he found the house, a man passed behind a porch support and stepped down to the drive. A wisp of gray bristle showed below a black webbed ball cap. He carried a small briefcase. The truck's front windshield pillar hid his face. After he sat, windshield glare did the same.

Black smoke shot from the tailpipe. Then he got out of the cab, pulled a thin stick or rod from the bed, and heaved it across Broadway. He got back in the cab. The truck backed from the drive and rocked to a stop at Broadway. "There he is," Lorenza Mercante said.

"There he is." Maytubby repeated. It was Steel-Toe, the second proctor at Foot Kingdom. The truck turned south on Broadway. "One of our Gomers."

Maytubby logged into a DMV database. "Tag stolen from Deaf Smith County," he said without looking up. Then he pocketed the phone.

"North wind at your back, Mr. Lighthorseman. You can catch him."

Maytubby hesitated, met her eyes. She knitted her brow and smiled, wagged the box knife toward the airstrip. "Go!"

Maytubby nodded, bolted out of the store, and sprinted to the Cessna. In the cabin, he shouted, "Clear!" and turned over the prop. He taxied a few yards to the center of the strip, pivoted by braking the right wheel, and shoved the throttle to the wall.

The tailwind carried him to the aqua truck on US 75 in short order. He throttled below the 125-mph cruise speed and hung a mile or so behind. Steel-Toe passed through the dead coal boomtown of Lehigh to Atoka, then Tushka, Caddo, Durant, and across the Red into Texas.

At the edge of controlled airspace for Dallas, Maytubby circled and picked up his field glasses. He was trying to avoid radioing Approach Control. At the end of the 360, he watched the pickup turn into the Sitka Auto Ranch.

Another semicircle and he was homeward bound.

He was flying low enough and slow enough to get cell reception. It was near sundown. Hannah took the call from her sumac blind, where she had just started her cruiser for the shift-ending trip back to Tish. "You fall in a clothes dryer?"

"Saw your prowler in the Blue lot off Seven. Season's over, Deputy." Maytubby added a little left rudder to better aim the plane's nose at the Ada VOR.

"You happen to see a black pickup in that lot?"

"I did. Guy with an orange cap."

"You follow him when he left?" Bond said.

"I left before he did," Maytubby said.

"What if he was fixin' to hurt me?"

Maytubby smiled. "I was too far away to warn him."

"Yeah . . . Well, mister, I found a clue."

Lake Texoma reflected a low red sun into the Cessna's cabin. Maytubby swiveled the sun visor to the pilot-side window and switched on the exterior lights. "Say on."

"Gas receipt from a Quik Trip in Plano. Dated Thursday."

"Hot biscuits, Hannah. You already call Scrooby?"

"Huh. After he sees the light, maybe."

"I think your friend Tiny peppered my plane with birdshot."

"That peckerwood. You musta been low. Any damage?"

"Don't think so," Maytubby said. "And I got a lot higher real quick. Listen, I followed a pickup that was leaving the Holy City just then. All the way to Coalgate."

"Didn't that fella that got burnt up on the Kiamichi useta—"

"Wiley Bates. Yeah. Same house, too." The evening air grew chilly. Maytubby turned up the cabin heat and added a little carburetor heat to prevent icing.

"That landlord must have a card on the outlaw bulletin board. Too bad the liquor store across the street's closed today. You coulda used that lady snitch."

"Lorenza Mercante," Maytubby said.

"That'n. 'Fore long, you're gonna have to put her on the payroll."

Maytubby thumbed the trim-tab wheel to add a little nose-up trim.

"She was workin' of a Lord's Day. Stocking. And she'd been watching Wiley's house already. By the way, the pickup I followed was the fifty-seven Chevy . . ."

"Steel-Toe." Hannah said.

"Yeah. Got a good look at him. Lor—Ms. Mercante says he's been stopping there regularly. Also, a black van or two with white lettering."

"Steel-Toe go to the car lot in Plano?" Maytubby heard cars pass Hannah on State 7.

"That he did. Before I followed him in the first place, though, I found fresh wheel ruts leading from a junkyard west of the Holy City right into Jerusalem."

"How far west?"

"Close. Next ranch." Though it wasn't dark yet, Maytubby could see the alternating white and green flashes of the Ada Municipal beacon.

"Old tin-roof house? Three chimneys?"

"Yep."

Hannah laughed out loud. "I served papers there Friday. Old baldhead slats named LeeRoy Sickles. Tiny Elephant's Ass is after a chunk of his property to expand the Holy City."

Maytubby couldn't see her, but her laugh was contagious. "Slats and Tiny." He snorted. "Toe to toe in Zion."

Maytubby heard Bond's turn indicator. She said, "Reckon I better check on my roommates."

He pocketed his phone, picked up the plane mike, and told Ada UNICOM he was entering the downwind leg of the traffic pattern. The runway lights were already lit.

CHAPTER 19

Bond's phone awakened just as she crossed Buzzard Creek. Local 580 area code. Not Maxine Fenton. "Johnston County Deputy Hannah Bond."

A voice whispered, "Deputy, this is Deb Laber." Bond heard a commotion in the background. "There's a man outside, pounding on the door and yelling something about 'mister.'"

Bond lit her strobes and stomped the accelerator. "Less than a minute out. Turn—"

"The lights are off, and we got a chair under the front doorknob. Jason's got his four-ten aimed at the door."

"Hang tight." Bond ended the call and pocketed the phone. Before she hit the Tish city limits, she braked sharply, turned off her strobes and headlights, and drove slowly. A half block from her house, she parked and pulled her Maglite from her duty belt but did not switch it on.

The shouting was high-pitched. Hannah took long, slow strides. She had heard more than her share of shouting as a child, and this didn't sound dangerous. Still, as she neared her yard, she laid her palm on the grip of her old Model 10.

She flicked on her Maglite and said, "Mr. Sickles!"

When he spun around, LeeRoy Sickles seemed to leave the ground. His arms flew over his bald head, and his eyes filled the lenses of his black-framed glasses. He still wore a T-shirt and overalls, had added a dirty ball cap but left the shotgun behind. "Oooh, goddamn," he cooed. He did his marionette dance.

"Deputy Bond," she said.

"Weellll. Tall Drink. I come to talk to you."

"How'd you find my house?"

He pulled off his cap, lowered his head, and shook it, like a dog. Then he said to the ground, "Asked folks. Who's in your place won't let me in?"

"Friends," she said.

Sickles slapped the cap against his palm. He sucked air through a grimace and wheezed a laugh. "Fraidy-cats."

"I'm telling 'em we're coming in."

He slid on his cap and tented his overalls bib with his thumbs. "How come you don't just go on in?"

Bond exhaled as loudly as Scrooby. She switched off her Maglite and said, "Deb, it's Hannah Bond! This fella's okay. I'll come in first." She stepped in front of Sickles.

The indoor lights came on. After a few thumps, the door opened a few inches. Sickles and Bond could see the chair wedged under the knob. Sickles said, "Looks like they're scared of *ever*body."

"It's stuck," Deb Laber said.

Bond said, "Stand back." She waited some seconds. Then she hit the door with her shoulder. There was a sound of wood splintering; the door flew open. Jason Laber stood beside his mother. His left leg was planted in front, his right behind. He pointed the shotgun at the floor in front of the threshold.

Bond kicked the chair kindling aside.

When Sickles saw the gun, he hopped back and flailed his arms. Bond turned and looked at him. He settled into small facial tics. "You don't have airn lock on your door, but there's a kid inside with a shotgun to blast yer nuts off."

Bond ignored him.

Deb Laber signed to her son as she said, "Unload the gun and lay it under the front window."

Sickles stuck out his neck and made googly eyes. "A *deaf-and-dumb* kid with a shotgun."

Jason did not see the old man speaking. He broke the gun at the breech, drew out the shell, and dropped it in his hoodie pocket. He eyed Sickles as he settled the gun on the floor.

Bond said, "LeeRoy, you and Deb stay put a minute. I have to return the squad car." She left the house and drove the cruiser two blocks to the courthouse, then walked home, checking the neighborhood.

When she came through the door and shut it behind her, she said, "I don't believe this table's ever been set." She waved her hand at three mismatched settings. Then she glanced at the iron skillet cooling on the stove. "Sergeant Maytubby buy them steaks?"

"Yeah."

Bond nodded. Jason stared up at her face. She sensed it and flicked her eyes toward him. He instantly looked down.

Bond said to Deb Laber, "Jason pays attention."

"*Too* good, sometimes." She tapped his shoulder. When he raised his head, she signed and said, "The deputy says you pay attention." He nodded once and looked back at the floor.

Bond said to Deb Laber, "Maytubby hardly eats meat. Or any regular food. I think he lives on raisins and cowpeas." She wrinkled her nose. "You and Jason go on and eat." She motioned to Sickles. "I need to talk to this fella in the bedroom."

* * *

Sickles and Bond stood on opposite sides of her twin bed. The room's only light was a single incandescent bulb in a bent sconce. It reflected on the bedroom windows and back-door pane. Semis on US 377 downshifted at the Tishomingo city limits.

Sickles fidgeted with his cap and rolled his eyes up to Bond's face. "Your place is awful tiny for a boardin' house, Tall Drink."

Bond tucked her thumbs into her duty belt. "Tish version of witness protection."

Suddenly still, the old man brushed his brow with his hat hand and frowned solemnly. "Oh," he said. "Sad for those folks. To get preyed on." Sickles looked at the patchwork quilt on the bed and then back up at Bond. "That boy's game, though."

Bond smiled just a little. "He is, Mr. Sickles."

The old man wrung his ball cap and said, "Deputy, I come over to report a theft on my property."

"Some miscreant dragged off one of your junk vehicles."

Sickles gaped. Then he sang, "Ooooh. Goddamn." The Morris dance resumed. He scratched his head violently. "You got a game camera out there or somethin'?"

"No."

He squinted and showed a few stained incisors. "You a witch, sister?"

"Yeah. I'm a witch. Do you know the make and model of the vehicle?"

He frowned and drew a cigarette out of his top overalls pocket. Bond opened a window and handed him an empty soda can from her dresser. His wood match flared in his eyeglasses. He blew it out. It plinked on the bottom of the can.

"Deputy, that junk pile's older than me. Woman I bought the house from said it started with the allotment Chickasaw who built the house back in territory days. But around the edges, where Tiny was poachin'—you know it was Tiny, right?"

"Looks like it," Bond said.

Sickles nodded and took in a lungful of smoke. "Around the edges was newer junk."

"How new?"

"Last fifty, sixty years." Sickles bent at the waist, stuck one leg forward, and swiveled on his pivot foot like a dervish.

"Was there a fifty-six Hudson Hornet in the new junk?"

Sickles ignored the soda can in his left hand and tapped ash on the floor. "I been there since it would've been junked, but I never owned one. I told some people from Tish and Sulphur they could tow their junkers in there. I wasn't always there when they did."

"Big vee in the grille? Chrome side molding?"

He looked up and to the left, tilted his head back, inserted his cigarette vertically.

Bond watched him march the soda can through the air, likely conducting his survey of the yard. Silverware clinked in the kitchen.

He lowered his head and grimaced as he shook it, hangdog. "Sorry, Deputy. I can't see it. And I didn't keep no inventory of the junkyard." He looked away and took a drag.

Bond unsnapped a compartment in her duty belt and removed a business card. She allowed the old man to look it over before she spoke. "If you see anything else suspicious out there, call the number I wrote in ink."

He took the card and slid it behind his cigarettes, raised an eyebrow. "You mean like a drunken orgy weenie roast?"

"No," Bond said, before she caught the gleam in his eye.

He squinted. "Hee-hee-hee-hee."

She shook her head and made a shooing gesture. "My meat's gettin' cold. Somebody will ask Tiny about the ruts on your property." Sickles was half through the door when she said, "Hey!"

He turned to face her.

"I'm workin' on this with a Lighthorseman sergeant named Bill Maytubby. Drives a gold-over-white sixty-five Ford pickup."

CHAPTER 20

Before Maytubby drove away from the Ada airport WiFi, he took out his phone and logged on to National Crime Information Center. Maybe Douglas Verner owned a vehicle other than the pickup his drunken wife had plowed into the rock pile. The pickup was in the county impound lot. The two new vehicles Hannah saw at his house had Texas temp tags—not likely his.

NCIC yielded no stolen or missing vehicle. At 8:40, Maytubby got out of his pickup, walked into the bright little terminal, plugged in his phone charger, and began calling small-town sheriffs and rural police departments near Tish. They likely would have matched any abandoned vehicle's VIN with the owner and contacted Magaw's office in Tish. If so, Maytubby would find out and skip this step. If the car had been found but not matched, he could go and look it over. If neither was the case, he would call rural service stations and groceries.

While he was listening to a deputy in southern Coal County tell him no such vehicle had surfaced in his bailiwick, Jill Milton's name appeared on his phone—an incoming call. Maytubby thanked the deputy, accepted his fiancée's call, and said, "Are you related to the blind English poet, author of *Paradise Lost*?"

"I never told you, because I wanted you to love me for myself."

"Is it okay if this sweetens the pot?" Maytubby looked at his reflection in the terminal's plate glass.

"Is it okay that the oldest known Milton in my family tree was a horse thief?"

"The famous 'inglorious Milton.'"

"The famous Abednego Milton. I'm guessing no *Ship of Fools* and leftover rutabagas tonight," Jill said.

"I have to conserve my vital force." Maytubby smiled past his reflection.

"I am a medical professional, and that is a myth. Besides, what are you going to do that requires abstinence?"

"Oh, I dunno," Maytubby said. "Run barefoot across miles of the Big Rock in the dark."

Jill was silent for a few seconds. "All right, Tarahumara. But if you don't wear sneakers at night, you can look forward to a long forever of abstinence."

"Even if I wear my Petzl headlamp?"

"You already stepped on one Choc bottle in broad daylight." Behind Jill's voice, a banjo negotiated Bach's Goldberg Variations. "What's on the Big Rock?"

"Lonely ranch-style house. Drunk woman who called me Tonto lives there. So did her husband, until sometime Thursday night. He's the guy that was floating in Pennington Creek. Doug Verner. He was having carnal relations with a woman."

"You mean, like, dancing?" Jill said.

"Baptist dancing. Her husband and the Tonto woman are both suspects. After the murder, Hannah checked out the house and saw expensive new vehicles there. Not likely his."

"Interlopers."

"Texas interlopers." Maytubby stood and stretched his left hamstring.

"Are you going to flush them?"

"Not if I can help it. Did you get that from old movies, or hunting quail when you were a kid?"

"I don't use no dead metaphors, buster."

Maytubby laughed. "You get that from the blind poet."

"And don't you forget it. Be careful on the Big Rock."

"Will do." Maytubby ended the call and resumed his inquiry. At 10:05, a clerk at Rob's Grocery in Fittstown told Maytubby someone had pushed a damaged car into Mill Creek off East 1660 Road a couple of nights before.

Maytubby stopped briefly at his house to change into torn jeans and a stained maroon hoodie. He found his raggedy camo ball cap and Petzl headlamp in a closet. He also took a set of goober teeth and a pair of taped-up low-power reading glasses from his dresser. He grabbed a sack of pepitas and dried cranberries and filled a workout bottle with tap water. His duty belt and field glasses were still in the truck.

* * *

A few pickups were still parked at Rob's Grocery when Maytubby drove past it fifteen minutes later. He slowed as he crossed Mill Creek, turned right on 1660 Road, and followed it until it veered away from the creek. There he stopped and slapped an LED beacon on the cab's roof. His truck was too old for hazard lights.

With his headlamp, he soon found ruts and flattened weeds leading to the car, its nose in the creek. It was a late-model Ford sedan. Its taillights and rear window were smashed out, and there were long, shallow dents in the trunk. Maybe a metal baseball bat. Not thin and rough like rebar. He took out his cell and photographed the car.

Its tag had been removed. "Stupid," Maytubby muttered. He slid carefully down the embankment, felt the chill stream cover his left sneaker. The windshield was also broken out. He brushed away glass cubes and photographed the VIN. He could memorize it, but the photo was needed elsewhere.

Back at his pickup, he looked up the VIN on his phone. The car belonged to the late Douglas Verner. Maytubby sent this fact, with a map and photos, to Bond, Magaw, Fox, and Scrooby. And he recalled that Verner's widow had said she fixed his wagon for good. Maybe she meant this—destroying his car, not murdering him. Or maybe whoever killed him did this.

In the cab of his pickup, he found a yard-long strand of crime scene tape, which he tied to the car's rear bumper. He took a pen from his pocket, flattened the tape on the bumper, signed his name, and wrote the time and date. OSBI would scour the car before Sheriff Magaw impounded it.

Ten more minutes down the highway to Tish, Maytubby turned west on Spring Creek Road and drove onto the Big Rock prairie. His headlights glanced off small mounds of gneiss boulders. Three miles in, he could see the Verners' yard lights in the distance. Hannah had told him the OSBI rookie staked out the house from the west, so Maytubby would approach it from the east. He found a track that crossed a cattle guard and headed south on it. At the bottom of a swale, he snugged the Ford into a Chickasaw plum thicket, pulled on the camo hat backward, slid the Petzl over it, and switched on the light. He dropped the hillbilly teeth in his jacket pocket. The pump 20-gauge shotgun bracketed on the roof of the cab was out of the question. He laid his palm on the duty belt. The Beretta would slow him down. He decided to leave it. The binocs he slipped into a jacket pocket, then disabled his camera flash. He ran a hand over his sneakers. There wouldn't be much glass this far from the road, maybe some burrs in the lawn. His soles were still tough from the last autumn running days. Off came the trail runners and socks. He locked the pickup, jumped into the wash, and jogged west.

The wash flattened onto plain. Maytubby freshened his pace, dodging rocks and deadwood, bending to keep the headlamp beam low to the ground. He startled a rabbit and a roadrunner, saw the hindquarters of a fleeing coyote in the cusp of his light. He crossed two small creeks, a rising wind soughing in the bois d'arc trees.

Half an hour, and the back of the house appeared. Two hundred yards. He turned off his headlamp, slid it into his hoodie pouch, and glassed the house. No visible cameras on the roof or walls. The foot doctor's security consultant hadn't made it this far afield. Most of the interior lights were on, shining through unshaded windows. He could see in; they couldn't see out.

He was in a buffalo wallow, beyond the sodium lamps' beams pooling on the grass. He took off the cap and mussed his hair, replaced the cap. The dark Escalade and the Titan, registered to Ella Bednar at Sitka Auto Ranch, were still in the carport where Hannah had seen them, but there were other vehicles at this rodeo. One was an old dark Dodge pickup. Hannah had told him Eliphaz "Tiny" Valentine owned an old Dodge. His friend Nail was connected to it, too. Maytubby had found their mugs online. The other vehicle was a new Porsche Boxster. It first looked white, an illusion created by the golden sodium light—very close to the car's yellow. His binoculars showed him that the decal and plate frame were both from Sitka Auto Ranch.

There was no ornamental shrubbery against the brick ranch-style. The empty flagpole lanyard pinged in the wind. Maytubby walked bent over between patches of thin cover—oak saplings, an abandoned chicken coop, a mower shed. The fifties-era storm panes on all the house's back windows were closed. He could have used his new lip-reading friends about now.

From the shed, he duckwalked to the carport. He smelled cigarette smoke. No one was standing at either back door—an encouraging sign. The porch light over the back screen door leading to the carport was dark, and the carport roof shaded the yard lamps.

When he reached the carport slab, he put the new vehicles between himself and the screen door, then stood up. Glad to be barefoot, he walked around the back of the Titan pickup and stood behind the Escalade. Through its tinted windows, he was looking into the glassed top of the storm door, at three men sitting around a kitchen table.

All were smoking cigarettes. A half-empty handle of brown spirits sat in the middle of the table. Every man had a small tumbler. There was one empty chair, with an empty glass on the table in front of it. All the drapes on the Spring Creek Road side of the house were drawn shut.

Maytubby recognized only one of the men, Jimmy Nail, from Hannah's description. Beside him sat a short man in a gray suit and red tie. Distance and window tint made him look like a possum. A metal briefcase was open on the table in front of him. Across the table from Nail, a dapper middle-aged man sat rigidly, his hands flat on the table. He wore round gold glasses and had a white streak in his black forelock.

Though Maytubby could make out few words, he matched faces with the pitch and timbre of the men's voices. The little possum had a rough bass voice. Nail was a baritone with just a trace of Indian in his voice. The natty man cleared his throat before he spoke.

Maytubby got to his hands and knees, gingerly circled the SUV, and stood in the shadow beside the screen door.

Someone sighed. Nail spoke. "Smoot said ten minutes. Whatchur shiny watch say, lawyer man? B'lieve I *will* help myself."

"It's been almost twenty minutes, Mr. Nail," Possum said.

A lighter flicked. Nail said, "So this Fenton dude fell outta the sky."

A throat was cleared. "After I tailed him to Nocona, Texas. That was just far enough. Time to snitch on his wife . . ." There was some muttering before he said clearly, " . . . late in the night."

Possum said, "Well, Tula knew her husband was screwing Fenton's wife a good while ago. So Fenton wasn't exactly tumbling from the firmament of heaven."

A chair creaked with strain. There was a long, low whistle. Nail said, "I'm not so sure your college pays protection for sayin's like that. Brad-ley."

The possum now had a name.

The throat-clearer's voice was placating: "Jimmy, we're gonna need this plan B. Now."

Nail was not placated. "No. Shit. I'm the one told you Tiny heard the cops talking about rebar!"

Nobody spoke for a half minute. Glass clinked.

Bradley said, "Using Fenton's yard gloves with his bat, Jimmy? Extra mile. Nice touch."

"Mmm," Nail said. He seemed placated now. "I took off that license plate and threw it in the Blue."

There was another long silence. Maytubby smiled.

The throat was cleared. "I wish Tula wouldn't of said what she did to the cops."

Nail said, "Add that to the new DUI, she won't be drivin' that new truck for a while."

Nobody spoke to this, but more than one of them hummed. Maytubby found the tunes jaunty, as if the men had just discovered "Maybe Never."

A chair scooted. Before Maytubby could hunker and flee, he realized that the lit room was reflected in the Caddy's rear side window. A ghost rose at the table. Instead of walking to the carport, it disappeared into the back of the house. The remaining two ghosts leaned together and muttered. He couldn't hear what they said.

A low roar came from the east. The Verner house stood between Maytubby and the source. Soon, he knew that it was a vehicle moving too fast for a gravel road. Smoot was late, so likely Smoot. Maytubby duckwalked around the Escalade and the Titan to the Titan's tailgate. The men at the table couldn't see him there. He stepped up onto the bumper and slowly scissored his legs over the gate, went on hands and knees in the bed.

The approaching vehicle skidded on the gravel and slewed loudly into the drive. Maytubby raised his head a couple of inches and snatched a glimpse of the '57 Chevy short bed. On the off chance that Smoot felt nosy, Maytubby put in his goober teeth and slid on his low-power readers.

The Chevy door boomed shut, and Smoot's soles crunched on gravel. There was commotion in the lit room; the storm door opened and shut. "Where's Nail at?" Smoot said.

Maytubby couldn't hear the answer. The wooden door slammed, and the carport went dark. Only underwater sounds from inside now. The Chevy's exhaust system pinged as it cooled. He could see the red Zia sun of a New Mexico plate—presumably stolen. A white Charger rolled slowly down Spring Creek Road. Scrooby's rookie. If one of the boys inside saw that car, the gang would vanish like steam.

Maytubby sat atop a side panel, pivoted, and slid to the ground. He walked slowly to the Chevy. Flash off, he photographed the tag in dim sodium light. He pulled the headlamp from his hoodie and held the Petzl inside the bed before he switched it on.

A spare tire was chained to a hole drilled in the side panel. Age and use had removed the bed's aqua paint, but except for a patina of dust, it was clean. No rocks or debris or twigs. Maytubby guessed it had been power washed. Even the gullies in the spare wheel were clean. He checked the carport door before he climbed into the bed, using his hoodie sleeves like mittens to keep his prints off. On his knees, he bent down and trained the Petzl on the seam between the bed and the side panel. He looked deep into the crack and moved slowly around the bed. A few glittering crumbs of silica, a few lodged sticks. The bed ridges hurt his kneecaps. For a power wash, the tailgate hinge would have been open, so he skipped that.

When he had almost completed the circuit, near the corner of the bulkhead between cab and bed, the headlamp caught some shiny streaks. Maytubby took out his pocketknife, opened it, and slid the long blade along the crack. It struck a light object. An olive Woolly Bugger. He left it in place. Inadmissible if he took it now. Through the rear window, he scanned the cab, which also looked as though it had been power washed. A pair of camouflage half-finger fishing gloves lay in the middle of the front bench seat.

Back on the ground, he found the Chevy's cab locked. He turned his back on the house and held the headlamp against the glass. He turned it on for the two seconds he needed to see the floor. His Ford ignition key was not there.

The old Dodge wasn't locked, and its dome light didn't work. On the dash, he found a balled-up PayDay candy bar wrapper, a Phillips screwdriver, and a wooden-headed mallet. Filthy bath towels covered naked springs on the seat. There were large rust holes in the floor. Also cigarette butts and empty soft packs of budget cigarettes.

The only large object in the bed was an upholstered armchair with no legs, its back against the cab. Large whitish arcs scored the rusted bed floor. Made by limestone blocks for the Holy City of Butcher Pen Road? The lamp caught a red glint close to Maytubby's hand. He tugged at his sleeve with the other hand and picked up the object, inspecting it in the shadow of the Dodge's side panel. It was an oval-cut acrylic ruby, with dried adhesive on its back. He left that in place as well.

The discovery had impaired Maytubby's hearing. The bang of the storm door registered just a second before he heard a loud real-time voice: Smoot's. "Let's have a look at Tula's ex-pickup!" The screen door thumped a few times. The last thumper switched on the carport light.

Maytubby froze, his back to the house.

Smoot said, "Jimmy, when's Tiny gonna pick up his Caddy?" There was no answer.

Slowly, Maytubby retrieved his cell phone. It was already muted. Amid the faint chatter from the gang, he slid his phone between the upholstered chair's attached seat and its back cushion. Then he edged along the truck bed toward the margin of the yard light.

"Shit!" one of the men yelled.

"Hey!"

Maytubby spun toward the men, who were not yet running. He widened his eyes behind the readers and grimaced broadly with the goober teeth. Then he let out a harrowing scream. One of the men tripped; the others faltered.

In the quiet beat that followed, Maytubby covered ten yards at a dead run. Now that he was in shadow, the sodium glow would work to his advantage.

A gunshot snapped. Then a second.

He ducked with each shot, then yanked on the headlamp. Westward he sprinted, away from his pickup. He vaulted a barbed-wire fence and found a cow path going his way.

Behind him, he heard some grunting at the fence, and at least two engines being revved. The fence guy, he could outrun. Satellite maps on his phone had shown a ranch vehicle trail just south of him, running east-west. A few seconds passed before headlights glowed in trees along Spring Creek Road. And very few more passed before the old Dodge's ancient suspension pitched a fit, the pickup closing on him along that trail on his left. Now headlights shone on sumac patches.

Both vehicles slowed. On Spring Creek Road, the white Charger sped back toward the Verner house, the rookie roused by gunfire.

Maytubby raised his head and aimed the Petzl first at the Dodge and then at the Chevy, so Nail and Smoot could see exactly where he was. Then he switched off the headlamp, slowed to a stop, did a military about-face, and ran toward his pickup. There was a moon. Maytubby hoped his pursuers would not turn off their headlights.

They didn't. He vaulted the cattle fence again but stayed out of the yard light. The Charger was stopped on Spring Creek Road, its spotlight playing over the front of the Verner house.

Maytubby made a hissing sign. He hopped into a dry wash to hide himself from the road, switched on the Petzl, and went hell-for-leather across the Big Rock.

CHAPTER 21

When Maytubby reached his pickup, Spring Creek Road was dark. He started the truck and left his headlights off, tossed back a few handfuls of pepitas and dried cranberries, drank deep from the sports bottle. Off came the disguise and the headlamp. He winced as he pulled a goathead from his heel. Then he slipped on his trail runners. As he backed onto the trail, sumac branches screeched against the sides of his pickup.

Driving slowly east, by moonlight, he reached a long straightaway. At the end of it, he could see no headlights behind him. He turned his on and accelerated.

* * *

The nearest cell phone vendor was a Walmart in Atoka. Maytubby drove much the same route he had just flown, across the Blue River Valley and through Wapanucka. State 7 wound between large forested hills before it flattened in the Clear Boggy Valley.

Under dazzling fluorescent tubes, Maytubby squinted at an array of no-contract phones. A teenage girl wearing a red Atoka Wampus Cats polo shirt clicked the phone case key against her front teeth. She stared over Maytubby's head. When Maytubby had found a phone he could use, he had to clear his throat to get the clerk's attention.

After she opened the case, Maytubby said, "Could you find the one that has the most juice?"

She gave him a moderate stink-eye and sighed. "They're all the same."

He nodded. "The guy who stole mine a half hour ago? He's fleeing a felony." The clerk's posture improved, and she lost the stink-eye. "I need to find my phone and him, and it may take a while."

She pulled out the bottom box and gave it to him. "I just finished charging that one. Are you a cop?"

Maytubby was cross-deputized in the Choctaw Nation, where he was now standing, but he didn't want to cause an international whisper incident. "Yes," he said, smiling. He paid for the phone and a data plan. "Can I use your bright light and Wi-Fi?"

She nodded vigorously, picked up a pen, and wrote out a network name and password. As she passed the paper across the counter, she leaned toward him and whispered, "It's for the managers. Secure."

He held up the paper and said, "That's very helpful, ma'am."

She flicked her eyes away and blushed. Maytubby went to work on the setup. The clerk ignored another electronics customer. Maytubby heard him clear his throat.

She watched Maytubby search for the phone-finder application. "This is so cool," she said. "What did he do?"

Maytubby lowered his voice to a whisper. "He might be part of a murder plot. I'm not supposed to talk about it."

The clerk made the halt gesture with both hands and shook her head. "No, no. I know. It's a legal thing."

He tapped "Install" and began scratching off the data card. The other customer edged down the counter toward them and cleared his throat more emphatically.

Maytubby said, "Okay, let's see where my phone is vacationing." He tantalized her by turning the screen a little toward her and then back. She leaned farther over the counter. "Looks like he's still on the road," Maytubby said.

The customer moved closer and said firmly, "Excuse me?"

The clerk turned to face him. Maytubby said to her back, "Thank you for helping me locate this app!"

She wheeled and shot Maytubby an incredulous frown.

He smiled and saluted her, then walked into Sporting Goods. The dot representing his phone inched slowly through Bromide, eastbound, then south into the woods bordering Butcher Pen Road. Near Tiny's house and the Holy City. Two minutes later, the dot moved back north toward Bromide Road before it left all named roads, roved a bit, and stopped. Maytubby toggled from map to satellite photo and saw, next to the dot, a large round structure with uneven walls, like the ruins of a castle tower or gun emplacement.

Before he left Walmart, he sent two texts. The first was to Hannah Bond: "*Maytubby here. My cell hitching with Nail. I fled Gautier gang at Verner house. Tailing Jimmy Nail south Bromide. Watch for Steel-Toe in Tish. Hunch.*"

The second was to Jill Milton: *"Call Monsieur Rutabaga at this secret number."*

The electronics clerk appeared at Maytubby's side, out of breath. "Where's the killer—I mean, your phone?"

"Strange place. Looks like an old castle. In the Forest of Wapanucka."

She looked at Maytubby and blinked.

"Really," he said.

She crimped her lips and crossed her arms. "You're blowin' smoke up my ass." She turned and took a step toward Electronics. Then she came around again and jabbed a finger at Maytubby. "And you're not getting anything!"

It was his turn to blink.

* * *

A big-truck air horn startled Maytubby as he was crossing the Clear Boggy. He glanced in his mirror before he saw the phone blinking on the seat. It was charging on the Ford's lighter port.

He accepted the call from Jill's number and said, "Exclusive Okra Produce. This is Bill."

His fiancée said, "There are rumors your company sells okra to anybody with ready money."

"Jealous competitors will spread untruths. You can view the framed certificate of exclusivity in our office. The state okra inspector audits us annually." A raccoon padded down the shoulder. Maytubby braked until it bobbed into the brush.

"*All* your products?" she said.

"Yes, ma'am. Fresh, frozen, breaded, gumbo mix, jelly, pickled, candy, soap, Santa ornaments, candles, hair conditioner, facial masks, flutes—"

"*Flutes?*"

"You heard right. We're the only manufacturer of okra flutes in the northern hemisphere."

A purple muscle car passed him as if the Ford were a slalom pole.

"The artisan lets the fruit grow as much as a foot before harvesting it."

Jill made a raspberry.

"It dries for a month. Then," Maytubby resumed, "following centuries of tradition, she trims away the thin end of the fruit and fashions an embouchure hole with the sharpened ember of a pawpaw branch."

"Hey, mister, my boyfriend's a cop. You don't find somebody else to lay your sick fantasies on, I'll turn him loose on you."

Maytubby clucked his tongue.

"So you're still in one piece," Jill said. "I'm putting you on speaker while I do dishes. Out on the Big Rock, you keep your runners on?"

"No. And for the record, I did need to steal up on my prey with catlike tread."

An owl ghosted across the highway.

"Did you tread on anything?"

"Yes. The pride of my adversaries."

"And?"

"A goathead," Maytubby said.

"That's kind of anticlimactic. You're driving, I can hear. Where are you?"

"Almost to Wapanucka."

"That's even more anticlimactic than the goathead," Jill said.

"You ask the wrong questions. Ask if I incited gunplay."

"Okay. Banter foul. That's too dark." The line was quiet a few seconds. "But it seems they missed."

"'Be' is the finale of 'seem.'"

Jill said, "Where is your phone?"

"I hid it in the back of an old Dodge pickup owned by a guy named Tiny." Maytubby slowed at the city limits of Wapanucka.

"Just happen to be a roll of bubble wrap back there? Otherwise, it's popcorn."

"I don't know why, but there's an upholstered chair fastened to the bed of the pickup."

"For Tiny's fares," Jill said. "What's Tiny's Christian name?"

"Eliphaz."

"Of course it is. Amish or Mennonite?"

"I don't think so. He's building a replica of the Holy City of the Wichitas on Butcher Pen Road."

"Ah. Church of the Manic Brotherhood." Maytubby heard dishwater sloshing behind her voice. "Is the Dodge holding still for you?"

Maytubby stopped at a blinking red light and turned north on Oklahoma 48. "For about ten minutes. Satellite view shows it next to a circular structure, kind of rugged—like the ruins of a castle tower—with some kind of roof."

"Or an abandoned cistern foundation."

"You empiricists suck all the romance out of life. It's not Tiny's primary residence. He lives in a shotgun house on Delaware Creek. He can see his new Jerusalem from there."

Maytubby heard a clatter on the line. "Last dish in the drainer," Jill said. "I finished the caponata tonight."

Maytubby threw back a handful of cranberries and pepitas. He heard the call switch from speaker phone.

"What are you eating?"

"Mahmohwee un punhun theeds."

She let him wash them down before she said, "What's your MO?"

"With any luck," Maytubby said, "the, uh, cistern tank foundation will have been converted into a storage building that contains vital evidence."

"What if it contains a pack of drunks playing five-card?"

"I'll create a diversion and then rush the joint."

"The man with the plan," she said, her voice trailing off. "If you're done late—or still working late—leave me a message."

"I . . ."

"Also," she said, "leave me a message if another guy with a pistol is coming over to kick down my door."

"I didn't . . ."

"I know. Go find your evidence, Sergeant."

He turned west on Bromide Road—one-lane dirt with volunteer hedges. Cleared pasture soon gave way to the scrub forest where his cell phone lounged. The truck shuddered over an abandoned railbed that once delivered KO&G passengers to Jazz Age spas in Bromide. He found a ranch trail leading south. It crossed an ungated cattle guard posted with a slug-splintered sign that said, "Prepair to Die or Keep Out."

CHAPTER 22

The red dot placed his phone two miles due south. Moonlight faded under the ragged canopy, and the summer satellite view on Maytubby's phone hid the trail beneath trees in full leaf. Two miles was a long way. His headlights wouldn't register for half that, so he shifted into low and drove the trail slowly, almost at idle.

He sighed, mussed his hair again, put the camo cap on backward, and slid the Petzl harness over his head. The glasses and goober teeth went into the glove box. He leaned forward and dropped his duty belt behind the seat. As the pickup jounced over ruts and rocks, he reached up and touched the shotgun in its bracket. This terrain was even rougher than the Big Rock, so he left his trail runners on. The goathead prick still throbbed.

The Ford's beams caught a possum and a skunk. Its springs and shocks whimpered. One mile out, he steered off the trail and stopped between two young post oaks, turned off the headlights, and killed the engine.

He might need a reason for trespassing at night. So he unlatched the 20-gauge pump from its rack. Three shells in the magazine tube and none in the chamber. He paused. The shells contained number 8 birdshot. Nobody hunted birds at night. He removed them, dropped them into his glove box, and fished out three slug shells, which he slid into the magazine tube.

His temp phone. If he ran into a snag, it would out him. He got out of the cab, pointing the gun at the ground, and hid the phone under a flat stone. Then he took his keys, locked the cab, and pushed them under the rock beside his phone.

Before he switched on his headlamp, he found the shaded moon so he could keep it on his right as he ran south.

The sound of crunching leaves under his feet, marking his stride, lulled him as he hewed to one of the trail ruts. Ten minutes in, he broke a sweat and breathed fast. Coyotes wailed in the near distance. The headlamp's beam jigged around the roots and stones. Maytubby judged his closing distance and was reaching to switch off the Petzl when a thick force slammed his back and sent him sprawling. The shotgun clattered away.

Fine edges of stone and twigs glowed close to his eyes. He planted his hands to raise himself, but he was dragged backward by his ankles, leaves and earth going up his nose and scouring his face. Something heavy jammed his face down, and he heard two crunching impacts to the right of his head, then the sound of the shotgun's barrel softly scraping stone. He smelled booze and cigarettes. The thing on his head, which he now understood was a boot, came away, and cold metal was jammed into the base of his skull.

"You do what I say, motherfucker, or I'll scatter your brains like chicken feed." A baritone voice with a trace of Indun, as Maytubby would have put it to Jill. Jimmy Nail. The cold metal left Maytubby's neck. He heard the pump-action shush and click as a shell was chambered. He was jabbed in his backbone. "Stand up and don't turn around." Maytubby obeyed. The headlamp was ripped from his head. He saw its light spin into the dark forest. "I'm too far behind you, so don't do nothin'. Also, I got a nine in my belt, and a work light in my pocket bright as noonday sun. Walk slow, straight ahead."

Slowly Maytubby's eyes adjusted to the night. Moonlight through the budding oak leaves gained a purchase on the sandy ruts. He put one foot before the other, suddenly feeling very hungry. He heard his captor's cigarette lighter rasp and saw the brief flare on dead leaves. On they walked, voiceless, for half an hour. There were no animal sounds, even in the distance.

A dull gleam appeared ahead of them. It gradually became a thin rectangle. Maytubby sensed his captor adjusting his clothing and the gun. When the light had become a window, the man said, "Put your hands up on that wall." When Maytubby had done so, a rotted door—more like a wide gate—squeaked open beside him. "Intruder comin' in, Tiny! Cover him in the front." The man backed away from the door and said, "You keep your hands up. Go inside. Slow."

Maytubby did so. He walked into a room lit by one gas lantern hung from a rafter. It backlit a huge man he assumed was pointing a pistol. There was a spool table with two metal folding chairs pulled away. On the table were a half-empty fifth of clear spirits, two glasses, and a ceramic bowl with cigarette butts and a bulldog pipe. The pipe was still smoking, and the room smelled like sweet drugstore tobacco and booze sweat.

The giant motioned to one of the chairs. He said, "Sit down." Maytubby took one of the chairs, directly under the lantern. Now he could see both men in the jaundiced light. A giant muscular, bearded man with snarled eyebrows, flowing white hair, and a mad prophet's eyes. Eliphaz Valentine, whose driver's license photo Maytubby had seen on Chief Fox's computer screen. And Jimmy Nail, straight gray-streaked hair down to his shoulders. Valentine stuck his pistol in the hammer loop of his overalls. He was wearing mammoth ratty brogans tied with baling twine.

With his right hand, Nail held the 20-gauge by the stock grip, at his waist, pointing it at Maytubby. With his left hand, he took a phone from his pants pocket and waggled it in Maytubby's face. "We seen you on our game camera. You read the sign? Or can you read? *Nunta chi holhchifo?*"

Maytubby was not a speaker, but he knew from his *ippo'si,* his grandmother, that he was being asked his name. He knitted his brow and said, "What?"

"What's your fuckin' name?"

"Ikkemotubbe." A Chickasaw character Maytubby knew from Faulkner novels. "Derek," he added.

"Huh." Nail seemed perplexed, as if he should know the name.

Valentine boomed, "What the hell you doin' on my posted property?" He took a limping step and reached for his pipe, pulled a box of matches off the spool table, scratched one to life, and sucked wetly at the pipe stem.

"Huntin' wild eatin' pigs," Maytubby said.

Nail brandished Maytubby's gun and said, "With a small-bore shotgun?"

"Slugs," Maytubby said.

"Watch 'im," Nail said.

Valentine pulled his pistol from the hammer loop and pointed it at Maytubby while Nail ejected a shell. He examined it and slid it back into the magazine tube. Valentine put his gun away.

"Twenty-gauge slugs. That's fuckin' low-rent, Ickie." Nail pulled a soft pack of cigarettes out of his jacket pocket with his left hand, stuck one in his mouth, and lit it from Moses's pipe.

Maytubby leaned over, clasped his hands, and bent his head down. Not so far that he couldn't search the room. It was littered with sledges and chisels, fast-food trash, and empty liquor bottles.

Against one of the curved stone walls, he caught a glimmer of colored points of light—blue, red, green, and white. He looked away.

"This ain't right," Nail said. Maytubby remembered what Hannah had said, and put Valentine and Tiny together. He heard a rasp on the floor and briefly glimpsed Nail's boot before the walnut stock hit him. He tasted pennies.

* * *

Faraway sounds of men laughing, somebody talking about the lantern, footsteps, and a rhythmic clicking and huffing that Maytubby dimly registered as air being pumped into a lantern tank. He remained still. The laughing resumed. His head throbbed, and through a squint, he saw dimly and double. He was looking up from the floor, at the spots of reflected color.

They were attached to a blurry wooden box atop one tall wheel and, presumably, another he couldn't see. The wheel had yellow spokes like an old carriage wheel. Without moving his head, he shifted his eyes to the front of the box. It sprouted two long shafts.

He was taken by a fit of nausea but stifled it before he vomited. His fingers were numb, and the room spun. He battled to lie still. He hadn't been spinning drunk since his college days at St. John's in Santa Fe. Deep breaths, enforced calm. Then a sharp memory of guilt for being drunk. He had followed a winsome recruiter to St. John's in defiance of his father.

A full hour passed, and the chill of unfloored earth tempted him to shiver. He fought it and squinted up again. His reason came back, and there the bastard was in all its glory: a Roman chariot for the staging of Tiny's passion play. The tumbrel for Doug Verner's corpse, leaving the treadless tracks across Deb Laber's land. The thing Jason had seen in the woods. Certain sure there was a silver plastic Roman helmet with a red plume lying in the bed of the chariot.

Maytubby felt restored, shut his eyes, and listened hard.

Tiny and Nail mumbled and laughed. Some country-and-western music, maybe from Nail's phone, wailed and twanged. A chair scooted back. The music stopped. Nail said, "We could easy take this fucker into the woods, shoot him under the chin with his gun, lay it under him, like he tripped and fell on it."

"Yeah, I guess," Tiny said. "He *was* trespassin'."

"And we got real business on our hands."

Tiny exhaled loudly. "That we do."

A klaxon-horn ring tone sounded. Jimmy said, "Yeah." There was a pause. "Yeah," he said. "You sure you got the right house, Smoot? How'd you find it?" Another pause. "Sounds right. You see any of 'em—the tall deppity, the mother, or the kid?" After a beat, Nail said, "Well, the deppity would see to it the blinds were shut. Okay. See you here when you're done."

Maytubby's left temple hurt like poison, and his left ear sang.

Tiny said, "I wished that kid hadn't of seen me. What the fuck was he doin' in the woods at all hours, anyway?"

Nail lit another cigarette. A glass clinked. He snorted. "Jackin' around. Who cares." He kicked a chair. "I want to know who took Smoot out the first time he went to get 'em. Smoot took down the plate number, but we got no way to trace it."

A match scraped, and Maytubby smelled the pipe tobacco mixed with cigarette smoke. Tiny sucked his pipe. He said, "Boyfriend or husband woulda parked in the yard. Smoot said that. He also said the boy musta told his mother, and she musta passed that along."

Nail said, "And now this jackass hog hunter shows up. He don't know shit about us. But we got to shut down everthing far and near after that snitch of a husband said he was goin' to the law." He kicked what sounded like a can. It clinked across the floor and hit Maytubby in the head. Maytubby stifled a wince.

"Okay, Tiny," Nail said, "you're stronger than me. Pick up that skinny Indun, and let's get after it before he comes to."

Maytubby shut his eyes and lay inert. He imagined being thrown over Tiny's shoulder and carried out into the woods. Maybe then he could twist free. But his captors had two guns between them. Sorry odds.

He heard Tiny's pipe clunk into its dish, both men breathing heavily. There were soft footfalls, and Maytubby felt Tiny's hands under his armpits. He remained limp as the hands grasped his belt and pulled him from the floor. His head rested on Tiny's chest as the giant grasped his ass and hefted Maytubby over his shoulder. Tiny stank of booze and sweat.

As they turned, Maytubby's hand fell against the handle of Tiny's pistol. He thought of Nail with the shotgun and the nine.

Nail said, "Let's go."

There were two seconds of silence before the shack door burst open and a deafening explosion shook the room. Chunks of wood fell from the ceiling. Tiny backstepped. Maytubby yanked the giant's pistol from the hammer loop and fell scrabbling to the ground. The room spun again as he sought balance on hands and knees and then rolled prone with the pistol pointed at Nail and Tiny. The smoky air smelled of gunpowder. Through the blue haze, Maytubby saw a skinny bald man in black-rimmed glasses, wearing overalls and a T-shirt and waving a blunderbuss.

Maytubby aimed the pistol at the ceiling and fired twice. Tiny and Jimmy Nail jerked their heads toward him. Maytubby saw the bald man break his twice-barreled gun and replace the shell he'd spent. Bald-pate grunted as he lifted the huge gun again. A grin overspread his face, and he shouted in a piercing tenor, "Drop that pump, long-hair! This here's a ten and it'll turn you and Tiny there into breakfast sausage."

Nail dropped the gun.

The bald man, twitching and nodding, said, "Grant it, Tiny there might be a little chunky. Hee hee hee."

Maytubby was confused. The bald man hadn't threatened him, so he rose, one limb at a time, finding his balance as he did so. He kept the gun trained on Tiny and Nail as he looked Nail over for the nine. Its handle stuck out of the back waistband of his jeans. Maytubby walked over, pulled it out, and slid it in his front jeans pocket. Then he walked clear of the two men, around to Bald-pate's side.

Bald-pate twitched and grinned, said to Maytubby, "Git the pump." Maytubby eased Tiny's pistol into his other pants pocket and picked up the 20-gauge.

The bald man said, "Tiny's big. I'd see anything in his pockets. Now, Long-hair—Jimmy, is it?—you empty your pockets in front of you." One of the bald man's twitches made the gun—and then Nail—jump. "Go slow."

Nail clenched his teeth and scowled as he threw cigarettes, a lighter, keys, and a cell phone on the dirt floor.

"Now, step back, Jimmy, and close your eyes." He nodded to Maytubby. "Get them keys and cover these buttholes with your shotgun." As soon as Maytubby took the keys and stood at the open door, the bald man shouldered his gun and blasted the phone. Tiny and Nail covered their faces with their arms and cursed.

The bald man again broke his gun, pulled out the spent shell, and reloaded. He quivered, grinned, and cackled, "Tiny, you pissant. Try to thieve my land. Steal from my salvage yard. You're 'bout as disabled as a worldwide rassler. Come along, Sergeant." Tiny and Nail stared at Maytubby, who was staring at the bald man.

Maytubby and the bald man backed out the door and continued backing until they reached the old Dodge. "Hop in," the bald man said, running to the driver's door. "Keys in the ignition. Those guys are dumber'n rocks."

Maytubby lowered his shotgun into the bed, hopped on the running board, reached into the chair in the bed and retrieved his phone, then held on while the truck fishtailed and headed back up the track toward Bromide Road. He swung into the cab and slammed the door. The 10-gauge muzzle rested on the floorboard by the stick shift. Maytubby gingerly steadied the gun's taped stock. The bald man clutched and ground gears as they bounced crazily over roots and stones. He said, "I walked up here from my place. You got a truck somewhere?"

"On this trail, a mile up. Who are you?"

"LeeRoy Sickles." His shoulders took turns jumping up. "That deppity—the tall sister . . ."

"Hannah Bond?"

"That's it." The truck glanced off a boulder. Its headlights flickered. "She served me a summons from Tiny's lawyer. Tiny stole some wreck off my property and I tracked her down in Tish. Found her holed up with a young woman and her deaf kid. The deppity said the woman and her kid was afraid and it might have somethin' to do with Tiny, told me to keep a eye on him. On my way home, I seen some headlights up here, so I thought I'd walk up. The deppity said she was working with a Lighthorseman. When I busted in, I figured that was you."

Sickles fought the steering wheel while he grabbed his pack of cigarettes from his pocket, shook one into his mouth, replaced the pack, and took out a box of wooden matches. Maytubby took the box from him, opened it, struck a match on the dashboard, and held it to Sickles's cigarette. He shook it out and threw it on the floor. "When we get to my pickup, come with me to Tish. When I was on the ground, I heard Tiny and Jimmy Nail talking on the phone to their friend named Smoot. He's outside Deputy Bond's house. Now I need to talk on my phone."

Sickles downshifted and gunned the engine.

* * *

"Bill?"

"Hannah, listen, Steel-Toe is outside your house. His name is Smoot. LeeRoy Sickles found me at Tiny and Nail's hang in the woods. Got me out of a jam with his elephant gun. We're on our way."

Maytubby ended the call before Hannah could respond. He scrolled through his messages to one from Lorenza Mercante: *"Lighthorseman, I have that thing the guy threw out of his pickup. It landed in the store driveway. It's a bumpy steel rod like you see around construction. I picked it up with a Kleenex, like in CSI. It's in the store in a bottle sack. Love, Lorenza."*

Sickles hit the brakes.

Maytubby's pickup shone in the headlights. He said, "Leave the lights on a sec. I need to get something." He retrieved his keys and the Walmart phone, latched his shotgun to the roof of the cab, pulled out the pistols and laid them on the floor, and started the truck. He turned on the headlights and watched Sickles back the Dodge off the trail and kill the engine and lights. Sickles got out of the truck with his shotgun and knelt for a few seconds at a front tire. When he got in Maytubby's cab, he laid the 10-gauge atop the dashboard, dangled the Dodge keys in Maytubby's face, and then stuck them in his overalls.

Sickles said, "I let the air out of that front tar. Those crooks can hot-war that pickup in the blink of an eye." He shut the door.

"Is the shotgun okay?" Maytubby said.

"Oh, yeah. The hammers is down." Sickles struck a match and lit another cigarette. He bounced up and down on the bench seat and giggled. "Hee hee hee. You see Tiny when I said you were a cop? That was the best thing in my life."

Maytubby shifted into first and hit the trail back to Bromide Road.

CHAPTER 23

Hannah Bond heard an idling engine and gravel crunching.

Before she could move, her cell awoke. She had been sitting in the dark at her table, facing her front door. A mug of cold coffee and her Steiner binoculars reflected streetlight. Her hand lay on her service revolver. She picked up the phone. Deb Laber sat up straight on the couch and pulled the top of her sleeping bag to her chin. Jason breathed deeply in his bag on the floor.

"Bill?" she said. Maytubby's voice on the phone sounded like a fly in the room. The phone's screen soon went dark, and she laid the phone back on the table. She picked up her pistol, saw that Deb was awake, and said softly, "We got trouble. Stay still a second." She walked to the door and slid the curtain aside with the barrel of her gun.

The '57 Chevy pickup was plain. Its engine had gone silent. Now a second car coasted in—a sports car with its lights off. If she shot Smoot through her window, it would be homicide. If she charged him and the other person, they might shoot her and leave the Labers defenseless.

Eph was the only county officer on patrol, and he was useless. Hannah called State Trooper Renaldo on his cell. After he said, "Hannah?" she didn't let him talk. "Jake, if you're close to Tish, get over to my house. Bill's coming in his pickup." She ended the call and pocketed her phone.

In the Chevy's cab, she saw a face illuminated partly by a cell phone Smoot had propped on the steering wheel, and partly by the streetlight. In the sports car, another face was suddenly lit by blue cell light. The possum. She pulled the pistol from the curtain, laid it on the table, and asked Deb, "Who reads lips better, you or Jason?"

"He does," Deb said.

"Wake him up."

Deb threw aside the top half of her bag and got to the floor. She touched the boy's shoulder. He lurched sideways out of his bag onto the floor, got to his knees, and stood up, gazing around. The golden sodium streetlight through the curtains was weak, but enough to see by. Deb took him by the shoulders and signed something. He nodded and looked at Hannah.

Hannah raised the Steiners and said, "I'll hold these binoculars so he can see the man in the pickup outside. I need to know what he's saying." She paused. "There's going to be dirty words."

Deb signed some more, and Jason nodded. Hannah walked to the door, holding the Steiners, and Jason joined her. She knelt down, squeezed the lenses close together, and lowered the binoculars to his face. Deb Laber got on her knees beside her son.

While Hannah took the weight, Jason grasped the barrels like a pro. Then she slowly pulled back the curtain.

Jason moved the Steiners slowly and then held them still. A battery wall clock in Hannah's kitchen ticked. Trucks downshifted on the highway. Hannah heard the boy holding his breath to steady the glasses. A minute passed. Jason took his right hand away from the glasses and signed to his mother. He moved his hand back to the binoculars. Deb said, "The man's not talking. He's texting."

"Damn," Hannah whispered.

Another two minutes passed. Hannah lifted the curtain and saw Smoot's thumbs move and then cease. He touched his phone with his index finger and watched it. The other car was dark.

A few seconds later, Jason said, "Aw. Awk."

Hannah and his mother moved their faces closer to his, like eavesdroppers. The boy was silent for many minutes.

Suddenly, he pushed the binoculars away, turned to his mother, and began signing furiously. Deb Laber nodded and nodded. Then she pulled him by his arm to the floor. She said, "All he could get was, 'Good you here now. After done. Gas. Follow. Cindy. Creek.' Then he saw the man hold up a pistol."

Hannah took a squatting step to Jason and patted him on his ribs. "Tell him good work," she said to Deb. Deb signed to him. Hannah said, "Now tell him to get his four-ten and load it."

Hannah could see Deb's eyes glisten as she looked up. Hannah said, "He's careful. He knows how to handle that gun." Deb raised her hands into the streetlight and signed. Jason did as he was told, and then knelt down facing a south window.

Hannah took her Model 10 and raised the door curtain with its barrel. Both vehicles were dark, their doors closed. The kitchen clock ticked.

In the distance, she heard a siren. Jake Renaldo would never be so foolish. Eph. Her neighbors had called the sheriff's office. She got on her phone and called dispatch. "Deputy Bond. Radio Eph and tell him to stay away from my house. Cancel the nine-one-one." She hung up, knowing it would do no good. The siren Dopplered up. She raised the curtain and saw that both drivers had gotten out of their vehicles and shut their doors to kill the cabin lights. They looked east, toward the approaching siren. Smoot reached in the back of his pickup and pulled out something bulky. He pointed to the man from the sports car and walked unevenly toward Hannah's house, one of his arms straight out for balance. She could see the gas can now. He set it down beside her house and ran back to his truck.

Eph was going to get himself shot. Hannah shook her head. To Deb, she said, "Wait. Wait." She saw Deb signing to Jason. Then Hannah opened a back window and tumbled into her yard. She grabbed the gas can and poured a little in her front and side yards before she tilted it over and drained the rest into her backyard. When it was empty, she put it where Smoot had left it, and clambered back in her window.

In the front room, Jason crouched with his shotgun's butt on the floor. When Eph's cruiser's strobes flashed against the curtains, Hannah took her pistol in hand and banged open the front door and screen. She strode into the yard and saw Smoot and the possum pointing their pistols at Eph, who was getting out of his cruiser. To distract the men, she fired two shots in the air and bellowed, "Eph! Get outta here!" Then she turned and ran to her charges. She heard two shots before she got in the door and propped another chair under its loose knob.

When Bond raised the curtain, she heard the cruiser's engine roar, its tires kick up chat. It lunged forward, smashed into the rear of the sports car, and drove it into the tailgate of the pickup. Porch lights popped on. The cruiser's strobes and one of its headlights showed Smoot and Possum clearly. Bond yanked back the door curtain and broke out the glass with the butt of her revolver. She knelt to aim at one of the men but saw house lights just behind both of them. They were aiming at Eph's cruiser. "Shit," she said. She fired two more rounds into the pickup bed. The men ducked, and the cruiser's belts screamed as it snarled into reverse. She saw it slash up her street, across the highway, and upend in the ditch on the other side, steam from its radiator billowing across a headlight. The men stood watching the crash.

"Good work, Eph," she said to herself as she duckwalked back to her duty belt for her speed loader.

"Quiet," she said to Deb, who did not need to sign to her son. Bond reloaded her revolver and duckwalked back to the door window. Her shots had their effect on Smoot and Possum. She glimpsed their heads above the pickup bed.

"There's two of 'em, Ms. Laber. They're gonna split up. One on each side of the house."

Her cell came alive.

CHAPTER 24

"Tiny sued me to get land for the Judas hangin' tree he wanted for his Bible town."

When Maytubby's pickup crested the last rise above Tishomingo, he looked at Sickles and saw the town lights make a golden line across his spectacles.

Sickles lurched in his seat and said, "He's on the dole, you know. Hee hee hee. A cripple. I shoulda shot him, back there." The town grew before them. "But you woulda put me in jail. Right, Sergeant?"

"Maybe," Maytubby said. "When we get back to the deputy's house, Mr. Sickles . . ."

"*Mister.* Ha ha *ha*. I think the deppity called me that. It means trouble."

Maytubby smiled and nodded and said nothing more. His temple burned, and his stomach growled. As they neared town, a line of brake lights blinked on and off ahead of him—far from the first stoplight on Main Street. Maytubby pulled into a church parking lot and called Hannah.

"Bill, don't talk. Smoot and the lawyer are in front of my house. I fired into Smoot's truck, and they're taking cover. They shot at Eph after he rammed the lawyer's sports car. He's in the ditch on Three Seventy-Seven."

Maytubby looked down the line of cars and saw the cruiser's strobes to the left. "I see it," he said.

"Good. You're close. Go behind my house. I figure they'll split up and each take a side of the house. All the porch lights are on. We don't want a farfight. Don't come up the west side. I emptied a can of gas there that Smoot was goin' to burn down my house with when he was done."

Maytubby steered back onto the highway. "LeeRoy Sickles is with me."

"He twitches, he'll blow us all to kingdom come. I'm callin' nine-one-one for Eph. When I call back, take it and don't hang up."

"Okay." Maytubby dropped the phone in his shirt pocket. To Sickles, he said, "We're going in behind the deputy's house. Two armed men are in front, taking cover from the deputy's fire behind a pickup. She thinks they'll split up."

Hannah called, and Maytubby touched the green "Accept" button and put the phone back.

"One on each side of her house," Sickles said. "That poor deaf kid and his mom don't deserve this."

"No," Maytubby said as he turned off his headlights and drove into the numbered street behind Bond's house. He killed the engine and said to Sickles, "We can't go on the west side of the house, because the deputy emptied a can of gas there the men were going to burn her house with."

"After they kilt everbody," Sickles said. His head jerked and then was still. "It's common." The cab was silent for a second. Sickles continued, "If one of those ass-wipes steps in there, I got matches." He pulled his shotgun off the dash.

Maytubby bent, picked up Nail's pistol from the floor, and stuffed it in his belt, behind his back. He shoved Tiny's pistol beneath the seat and unlatched the 20-gauge from the roof. "LeeRoy, we're in town, and everyone is scared and looking out their windows. We can't shoot bystanders."

"Got it. But they can." Sickles rolled out of the cab and held his gun high across his chest, like a quail hunter. Maytubby opened his door and pointed his shotgun at the ground. There was no cab light, so the doors hung open. Sickles and Maytubby came side by side, treading slowly toward the dim sconce bulb in Hannah's bedroom.

Hannah said on Maytubby's phone, in his pocket, "They ain't budged." A siren whooped from town: Eph's ambulance. "Wait. Hold on. They're comin' to the front."

CHAPTER 25

On hands and knees, Hannah went to the window in front of Jason, raised the blinds, and threw open the sash. She shouted to Deb Laber, "Tell Jason to shoot at the ground through the front window."

As Hannah scrambled back to the door, she saw Deb signing. She raised her pistol and fired at the ground. A second later, the .410 boomed. Smoot and the lawyer retreated.

"Bill, me and the trapper sent the bastards back to the truck," Hannah said.

CHAPTER 26

"Okay," Bill said to his pocket. "I'm coming on the east side, Sickles on the west."

"Stand near the house," Maytubby said to Sickles. "And get your matches ready. You know what to do." Sickles reached into his overalls pocket with his left hand and took out the matches. His right hand held the blunderbuss stock upright against his hip.

Maytubby toed off his trail runners, then paced slowly east, away from Bond's house. He traced shadow from the streetlight. First, he saw the damaged sports car, then the old pickup. When he reached Bond's street, he could see Smoot and the lawyer, Bradley, behind the truck. He heard their hoarse whispers.

Stooping, he took one slow step after another and saw the place where shadow gave way to streetlight, just before him. The men raised their pistols and faced opposite directions. Maytubby stood and raised his shotgun. Stepping into the light, he said, "Drop your guns!"

Then Bradley spun toward him, wide-eyed, and dropped his pistol. Smoot ducked and ran around the front of the pickup and toward the house. Maytubby picked up Bradley's pistol, threw it as far as he could toward Bond's house, and said, "Lay down. Now!"

Bradley got on his hands and knees while Maytubby sprinted after

Smoot. He had not gone ten yards before he heard a concussion and felt an inrushing draft between his legs. A wall of flame silhouetted a figure running toward him. Maytubby recognized Smoot, hit him in the jaw with the shotgun stock, and then pulled him away from the flames.

The jouncing form of LeeRoy Sickles, holding his 10-gauge aloft, followed Smoot out of the conflagration. "Oooh, got*damn* that was fun, Sergeant," he said, planting the butt of his gun on the ground.

"Hannah!" Maytubby yelled. "We got 'em! Come out!" He dragged Smoot behind the pickup and walked across the road so he could cover him and Bradley. The flames ignited shrubs and licked at tree limbs between Bond's house and the Labers' car. Maytubby heard a siren from downtown—likely the fire department. Hannah emerged from the house, her revolver pointed at the ground. Deb, with her hand over her son's shoulders, followed her. Jason was unarmed.

Hannah turned and said to them, "Wait here. You're safe now." She turned toward the pickup and joined Maytubby behind the prisoners. Smoot groaned. "Your cuffs are in the pickup?" she said to Maytubby.

"Yeah, and yours are in the house. Watch these guys and I'll get mine first."

An Oklahoma Highway Patrol car pulled up beside Maytubby, its passenger window down.

"Jake!" Maytubby said.

Renaldo said, "Hannah called. You need help?"

"I think we got it, Jake. Thanks. You speedin' much?"

"One-forty, down on Seven."

"Phoo-*ooo*!" Maytubby said. Renaldo laughed as he drove away.

The Tishomingo Fire-Rescue brush truck skirted the ambulance tending to Eph and rumbled behind Bond to get to the fire.

After Maytubby returned, he cuffed Bradley on the ground while Bond retrieved her duty belt in the house. She took the cuffs from it and buckled it, with her Model 10, around her waist. Smoot had almost come to when Hannah sat him up and put the handcuffs on him. He had bled from his mouth over his shirt. "You're gonna need a couple new teeth," she said.

Fire-Rescue hosed down the blaze in minutes. The team mounted their truck and left. By now, all the porches in the neighborhood were full of the curious and worried. Hannah turned to the houses on her street and shouted, "All over, folks. Please go inside." Some did, and some stuck around to see what would happen next.

Bond read the prisoners their rights. Maytubby stayed to watch the men while she walked back to Deb and Jason. She noticed LeeRoy Sickles angling to join her.

When the four were together, coughing from singed grass and leaves, Hannah holstered her revolver and said to Deb and Jason, "You done good. You can pack up your stuff and go home now. I think we got the feller who came at your house."

In the streetlight, Deb began to sign to her son, but he nodded and waved her off.

Sickles knelt to Jason and turned his face into the streetlight. He said slowly, "I heerd your gun, boy. You're salty."

Jason turned to his mother. She clarified the "heard"/"here" ambiguity by pointing to her ear. For the second part, Deb looked at Hannah. "Tough," Hannah said. Deb signed that to Jason. He looked away shyly.

Deb Laber spoke to Hannah. "You and the Lighthorseman saved . . ."

Hannah had already turned toward the truck.

CHAPTER 27

While Maytubby watched the prisoners, Bond walked toward her cruiser at the courthouse. On her way, she called Mercy Hospital in Tish and asked about Eph. She was told he was still in the ER but had not been shot—was having glass fragments extracted from his face and torso.

Bond drove the cruiser back to her street. She parked next to the prisoners and got out. Maytubby opened the back door of the cruiser. Bradley was still lying prone on the blacktop. Bond grabbed the collars of his shirt and sport coat. She lifted him into the air with one arm, carried him to the cruiser, and stuffed him in.

Maytubby said, "We should take Smoot to Mercy."

"Who's gonna watch him? Eph's there, too. And we have to go up in the Bromide hills and get *those* bastards."

"What about Katz?" Maytubby said.

"You think he's back from the Monster Trucks?"

"Oh, okay," Hannah said.

She called his cell. He was on his way back to Tish. "But I drank some beers."

"More'n' four?" she said. "Never mind. We need you to sit a prisoner named Smoot at Mercy." She thought a second and added, "He's dangerous."

"Phooo-*ooo,*" Katz said. "I'll be there in a jiffy."

"Drive careful, Deputy," Hannah said. But he had ended the call.

Hannah put her phone away and turned to Maytubby. "He's on his way, but he may be half-drunk."

They carried Smoot to her cruiser, drove to Mercy, uncuffed and unloaded him at the ER. They waited until Katz arrived, amped and officious, and then they drove Bradley to the Johnston County Jail for booking. When they left the jail, Bond said, "You think my cruiser can get over the territory in Bromide?"

Maytubby said, "Maybe some high centers, but yeah."

Bond drove very fast. She handed Maytubby some jerky, which he gnawed with relish.

When the cruiser spun onto State 7D, she said, "Tell me where to go."

Four minutes later, they bumped over the cattle guard on the trail Maytubby had left less than two hours ago. Bond switched off the strobes and her headlights and slowed to a crawl, navigating by pale moonlight under mostly bare trees. Maytubby told her he was texting Jill. When he finished, he put his phone away. His pump's muzzle rested on the floor against the passenger door. He had pulled Nail's pistol from his back waistband and slid it into his front pocket.

"Hannah, let's stop here."

She switched off the ignition.

"Tiny's truck is just up ahead. Sickles let the air out of one of the tires. He kept the keys but said they would hot-wire it."

Hannah nodded and said, "That old joker is nobody's fool."

"No," Maytubby said.

"I got my Maglite in my belt. And plasticuffs."

They opened the cruiser's doors gingerly and stepped onto the leaves and stones. The dome light was decommissioned, so they left the doors open. Bond drew her revolver, and Maytubby set his shotgun across his chest. They stood still for long minutes, listening.

Some coyotes yelped in the distance, and from miles above them came the faint growl of jetliners bound for Dallas and Miami.

Then a metallic *toc* and muted human voices. Hannah took the first step. Maytubby walked beside her. They set their feet softly, keeping to the ruts. The voices grew louder as they approached.

A swinging light appeared. They halted. Someone said, "You ready?"

An engine chuffed and then roared to life. There was a bang and then the sound of a door slamming. Maytubby and Bond raised their weapons. With her free hand, Bond slid the Maglite, switched off, from her belt and held it beside her head.

Two dim headlights flicked on.

Maytubby said, "Wait, Hannah. Let's step off the trail." They backed a ways into the brush.

There was the sound of gears grinding, and the truck lurched forward. Its headlights bounced, and its suspension grated. A few seconds later, it lurched to a halt. Doors creaked open, and the swinging light crossed in front.

Someone yelled, "Got*damn*!"

Hannah said, "Right, let's go."

Bond and Maytubby jogged toward the old Dodge. Its engine drowned out their footsteps. When they were close enough to see Tiny and Nail inspecting LeeRoy's handiwork by lantern light, Bond switched on her Maglight, and Maytubby shouted, "Get down on the ground right now!"

The men turned to Hannah's light and squinted. Maytubby fired his 20-gauge into the air.

Both men fell prone, and the lantern Nail was holding tipped toward him and spilled flame along his hand. He flapped his hand in the dirt. Maytubby picked up the lantern, stomped out the flames, and shut off the gas.

Bond snapped open a holder on her belt, pulled out two pairs of plasticuffs, and tossed one to Maytubby. She knelt on Tiny's back, yanked his arms around, and cuffed him. Maytubby did the same with Nail. Bond stated the reason for the arrest and gave them Miranda.

She picked up her light from the ground, rose, and shined it on the two suspects and Maytubby. Maytubby pushed off Nail and stood beside him. The men on the ground panted. Maytubby looked at the truck, and Hannah said, "Yeah, one of my burn-in-hell foster dads showed me how to turn off a hot-wired car, but let's leave it to run outta gas. Garn can tow it tomorrow. It'll have prints. Take my light, and I'll go fetch the cruiser."

After she had handed over the light, Nail yelled at the ground, "You're not gonna last the night, neither of you. You got no idea who you're fuckin' with."

"Hush," Tiny said.

Nail lifted his head from the ground and turned to face Tiny. "Screw you, old man. You don't run this thing. You're dumb as a pump jack."

The cruiser stopped behind them. Its headlights lit the scene. Hannah got out and walked toward the men. She said to Maytubby, "I called the Assistant DA. He okayed a warrantless arrest. I left a message with Scrooby."

Maytubby nodded and lowered his head. "Who are we messing with, Jimmy?"

"Ha!" he said, testing the cuffs. "I ain't stupid like Tiny."

"Do you mean Smoot? We're messing with Smoot?" Maytubby said.

"I never heard of nobody named that," Nail said.

"Old Possum Face, the lawyer," Hannah said. "What's his name, Sergeant?"

"Bradley," Maytubby said.

"Yeah, *Brad*-ley," she minced. "Are we messin' with *him*? *He* gonna kill us?"

"You got-damned sow!" Jimmy kicked his legs.

"Shut up," Tiny said.

Maytubby said, "If Smoot and Bradley are going to mess with us, somebody will have to break them out of the Johnston County Jail." He paused to hear the silence. "How deep's your bench?"

"*What* fuckin' bench?" Nail said.

CHAPTER 28

When Maytubby walked into Jill Milton's garage apartment on Kings Road, she said, "You smell like Coleman fuel and gun smoke." She squeezed him around the waist and kissed him hard. Then she pulled his hoodie over his head and threw it on the floor. "I have a pot of sailor beans and a skillet of jalapeño cornbread. Take a shower." She was wearing a plum boatneck sweater and Levi's.

"Can I have some cornbread?"

"Only if you strip first."

When she turned toward her tiny kitchen, he peeled off all his clothes, picked up his hoodie, and carried them all to her stacked washer-dryer. He put his clothes in the washer, added some soap, and shut the lid. She appeared beside him with a slice of buttered cornbread on a saucer, and a glass of Chardonnay. He devoured the cornbread, holding the saucer under his chin and filling it with crumbs.

"Hannah didn't feed you?" Jill said.

Maytubby held up a finger while he washed down the cornbread with wine. He tossed his head back and shook his thick black hair. When he lowered his head and looked at his fiancée, he said, "Jerky. Long ago." He took a long draw of wine and handed the glass and plate back to Jill. "Shower," he said, and turned.

She set the wineglass on the saucer and then slapped his bare ass.

When Maytubby stepped out of the acrylic shower stall, Jill tossed a bath towel onto his head and rubbed his hair. "You have a knot on your head," she said. She was naked. Outside the bathroom, the only light was a candle burning on the kitchen table. She toweled him all over and took his jaw in her hands. He swept her into his arms and carried her to the couch. They fell on its back, upset it, and made love on the back cushions.

When they were spent, panting and slick with sweat, they laughed in the silent room. Rafters in the old roof popped, and the water heater clicked on. Jill said, "How about some beans and a banjo serenade?"

"You been readin' too many romance novels, girl."

Jill rested her head on his neck and said, "True. All your fault—you got me started on that *Ship of Fools*."

"Gateway romance."

"I'll say. Dreamy young German doctor," she said.

Maytubby took a sheaf of her hair in his hands and let it fall down her arm. "With a fatal heart condition."

"Beautiful and world-weary Spanish activist."

"Who's a morphine addict, supplied by the dreamy doctor."

"All in the Harlequin toolkit," she said.

"Embittered coquette, rapist ball player, Nazis, starving peasants in steerage."

Jill pulled his earlobe. "But it's a moonlit cruise from sunny Mexico."

"To prewar Germany."

"As I understand the craft of romance," Jill said, "the author is urged to inject realistic detail."

"I see. And this explains why you have offered your sinewy paramour navy beans and a banjo serenade."

"Yes. Those are the only things a poor working girl like me can offer. They will be enough to secure a proposal from her man." The washing machine clutched into its spin cycle.

"We've already proposed to each other," Maytubby said.

Jill stood and took his hand. "See there?"

He rose and kissed her shoulder. They walked into her bedroom. She slipped a navy sleepshirt over her head and went back to the kitchen. Maytubby found his clean running sweats in the top drawer of her dresser. On his way to the kitchen, he moved his stalking getup to the tiny overhead dryer.

A little pile of greens and a red pepper sat on a wooden block on the counter. Jill slid a bowl of beans into the microwave and said, "Chop and shred, my sous chef." She handed him a weathered chef's knife, and he went to work.

They sat in candlelight at her drop-leaf table and clicked spoons in the air.

Maytubby demolished a bowl of beans and two pieces of cornbread, then took a deep breath and downed half a glass of Chardonnay.

"That's impressive," Jill said. She forked a bite of salad and then took a spoonful of beans.

Maytubby sat back in his chair and shook his head as if to clear it. His temple still throbbed.

"That knot on your head is getting bigger," Jill said. "And you have a spreading bruise. You want some ice?"

"Good idea." He rose, went to her refrigerator, and took out a plastic tray of cubes. He broke them into a kitchen towel and applied the pack to his head.

"Should I ask about the boy and his mom?"

Maytubby sat at the table. He said, "Jason and Deb Laber. Hannah saved them by taking them in at her house. Tonight, the guy who came at the Laber house in Mill Creek showed up in Tish with one of his creeps and made a run at Hannah's house."

"Unwise," Jill said.

Maytubby set his elbow on the table. "Always," he said. "Those creatures are in Johnston County lockup. Jason and Deb have gone home."

"Good," Jill said. She watched him as she broke cornbread into her bowl of beans and sipped her wine.

Maytubby spoke softly. "Tell Fran Overton she helped us break the case."

"I will." She took a bite of beans and cornbread. "And?"

"After that, Hannah and I paddled into the heart of darkness south of Bromide."

Jill smiled wickedly. "I'm afraid to make a joke about Mistah Katz."

Maytubby chuckled and then winced, coddling his head. "He's not dead. But Hannah and I waylaid two other desperadoes there and put them in Tish, too."

Jill sipped her wine. "And their enterprise?"

"Medicare and Medicaid fraud in Texas. They were in cahoots with a Dallas podiatrist who—"

Through a mouthful of food, Jill said, "Wawyyt. Paww*di*atrist? A *foot* doctor?"

"And a member of our tribe."

Jill sat up and swallowed.

"He recruited patients, some through the tribal network, so he could bilk the federal government for surgeries he never performed."

"And someone was *killed* over this?"

Maytubby finished his Chardonnay and, with his free hand, carried the glass to the sink. "A snitch," he said. He returned to the table and sat down heavily. "But I don't think the snitch knew about the operation. He was going to tell Medicaid administrators about the crazy old man on Social Security Disability I told you about—the guy who is building a replica of the Holy City of the Wichitas."

Jill said, "The funny Bible name, but called Tiny."

"Yeah, Eliphaz."

"How'd the snitch know about Tiny?"

"His wife was in the ring," Maytubby said. "She was the drunk woman who crashed her car and called me Tonto."

Jill finished her salad and beans in silence and took her plates and the wine bottle to the kitchen counter. Maytubby followed her, dumped out the ice from his compress, and pulled up the sleeves of his sweatshirt. Jill ran hot water into the sink and poured in some dish soap. She split the last of the wine between them and sank the saucepan and dishes into the dishwater. They stared at the sink.

Jill picked up a dish towel and held it. "So Tiny is a kind of cracked visionary, a folk artist who cheats the system so he can realize his dream. I get that."

"But it's not greed, not a lust for money," Maytubby said.

"Right. Then what made him league up with these depraved assholes?"

Maytubby took a dishrag from the window ledge and started washing the dishes. "I don't know. May have been a crooked doc in Tish. More likely, he hurt his foot, and his low-life Chickasaw pal Jimmy Nail steered him to the corrupt Dallas podiatrist."

"And he was sucked in." Jill opened the cold tap, rinsed Maytubby's clean dishes, and set them in the drainer.

"That part will be a job for the Texas attorney general's Medicaid Fraud Control Unit."

Jill set the last dish in the drainer and dried her hands. "What about your chief Fox and Hannah's sheriff . . ."

"Magaw."

"And that state guy named after the Puritan town."

"Scrooby." Maytubby dried his hands. "Hannah called Magaw and got him to the Johnston jail after the second two were booked. Magaw is supposed to persuade Scrooby to come down from the City in the morning. I called Fox and tore him away from his beloved *Bass Masters* on cable. He groused but agreed to go to Tish."

"Up with the chickens for you, then."

"Yes." He walked to the couch and lifted it upright.

"Sure you're not concussed?"

"There's only one of you, and the floor isn't tilted. So maybe not."

Jill blew out the candle. They joined hands and walked toward her bedroom. "You know," Maytubby said, "all this ruction and heat over one lost life." He swept his hand into the air. "You and your diabetes education crew will save thousands of lives."

They stopped at the side of her bed. Jill yawned. "Perspective is so dull, Willie," she said in her world-weary Spanish condesa's voice.

Maytubby smiled and switched off the light.

CHAPTER 29

Hannah Bond was leaning against her cruiser, arms folded over her chest, when Maytubby drove into the Johnston County Courthouse lot. Chief Fox's Lighthorse cruiser and an OSBI car were parked nearby. Some crows pecked at gravel in the alley. The air was thick with Gulf wind.

Maytubby had left Jill's apartment well before dawn, gone to his house, and changed into his uniform. He had driven his pickup to the Johnston County impound lot. Garn was just lowering the old Dodge from his wrecker. Smoot's pickup was already in the lot. Maytubby snapped on disposable gloves and took evidence bags—two plastic and one paper—from his duty belt. Garn was unchaining the Dodge when Maytubby greeted him.

Garn nodded. "Bill."

"I got to make a quick inventory," Maytubby had said.

Garn knew the drill. He leaned against his wrecker and sucked on a toothpick.

Maytubby quickly retrieved the Woolly Bugger from the bed of Smoot's pickup, the acrylic ruby from the bed of Tiny's truck, and cigarette butts from Tiny's cab. The butts were still damp, so they went in the paper bag. He gave Garn a little salute and drove away.

Now Maytubby walked to Hannah, carrying Fran Overton's interview notes and the evidence bags he had just filled. He also held five ripped-out pages of the *Oklahoma Atlas and Gazetteer,* folded tight.

Bond said, “Nice shiner.” Then she eyed his papers and bags.

When he stood next to her, he said, “Yeah, the evidence. I know.”

She shook her head. “Scrooby’s mad as a wet owl.”

Maytubby held up the clear bag with the trout fly. “This’ll settle his hash.”

Bond chuckled. She looked across downtown Tishomingo. “You know how ridiculous this is going to sound?”

Maytubby nodded. “I do.” He let his arms, and his evidence, fall to his sides. Traffic idled at the highway stoplight. “Hannah, one thing I overheard at the Verner house. Bradley—Possum Face—praised Nail for using Fenton’s yard gloves with the bat to hammer Doug Verner’s car. You talked to the Fentons.”

Bond frowned and looked down. She uncrossed her arms, made her left hand into a fist, and gently thumped the fender of her cruiser. Her eyes searched the ground, then rose and scanned the horizon.

The back door of the courthouse opened. The dispatcher looked around it toward Maytubbby and Bond.

Bond stomped her right foot and said, “Shit!” The dispatcher stared at her.

“Bill, I plumb ignored it. Ms. Fenton—her first name is Maxine—said somebody broke into their shed.”

“Not quite so ridiculous now,” Maytubby said. He stuffed the bags and papers in his pants pocket and said, “I think we are wanted inside.”

CHAPTER 30

OSBI Agent Dan Scrooby leaned over an open Styrofoam takeout box, shoveling his breakfast with a white spork. Bits of scrambled egg hung on his black uniform jacket. He was the only person sitting at a Formica table in the conference room. Chief Fox and Sheriff Magaw, both lean men, stood beside the table and sipped from plastic mugs. The room smelled like sage sausage and burnt coffee.

Fox and Magaw nodded at Maytubby and Bond. Then they all stood without speaking while Scrooby's utensil squeaked against the container. The squeaks grew louder and more urgent as he neared the bottom of his feed. When he had finished, he threw his spork into the container, wiped his mouth with a paper napkin, shut the box, and exhaled like a surfacing whale. He drained a cup of coffee and then looked wearily around the room.

"Bill," he said. "Who blacked your eye—Tula Verner?" He looked at Bond. "And *Wilma*, if I'm not mistaken. Wilma Handue."

Bond stared him down.

"I've got a possible kidnapping in Kingfisher County, so this better be good." Scrooby pushed away his box but did not stand. He looked at Maytubby. "Sheriff Magaw and the OSBI have a solid suspect. Curt Fenton had motive and opportunity. He learned that Mrs. Fenton was screwing the victim, and he was back in Tish from a sales trip." He paused and looked up at Bond. "Agent *Ca*ble, Deputy Bond, found two gardening gloves and an aluminum baseball bat near the victim's abandoned and vandalized vehicle near Mill Creek. He showed these to Maxine Fenton, who identified them as belonging to her husband. She claimed the outbuilding on her property had been broken into. Agent Cable also found a length of rebar near the victim's car. It has stains that have not been analyzed. Mrs. Fenton has confessed to having an affair with the victim, Douglas Verner." Scrooby opened his hands and then clasped them together. "Simple small-town adultery revenge." He belched with his mouth closed and then surveyed the room. To Fox, he said, "The body was found on tribal land, but the murder was not committed there. I see no reason for you and Sergeant Maytubby to be here."

Chief Fox said calmly, "Sergeant Maytubby and Deputy Bond may have uncovered some useful information."

Scrooby twisted his head to face the sheriff. "Benny, did you assign Deputy Bond to this case?"

"No sir," Magaw said, his face a little drawn.

Scrooby began, "Well—"

Magaw interrupted. "Hannah has been known to take things into her own hands."

"Yeah," Scrooby snorted. "I've noticed."

Magaw frowned, scratched the back of his head, and interrupted again. "Show initiative, I mean."

Bond looked at the sheriff. Maytubby glanced sideways at her to catch her surprise. He failed.

Scrooby opened his hand and ran it back and forth over his thinning hair. He exhaled and looked at his watch. "Five minutes," he said, and covered his eyes with his left hand.

Maytubby and Bond walked halfway around the table so they faced Scrooby. Bond kept her arms crossed and looked down at the agent like a cruel matron. "Fenton's a fall guy," she said. "Doug Verner was gonna snitch on his wife's hoodlum buddies. He feared 'em. They all knew he was pokin' Mrs. Fenton, so they had their mark. Made it look like—whadja say?—a 'small town adult'ry revenge.'"

Scrooby's eyelids were heavy with the meal. He strained to find Bond's face against the fluorescent tubes overhead. "By 'hoodlums,'" he swept one arm toward the jail wing, "I assume you mean the jackasses takin' up Benny's cell space."

"Yeah, I do," Hannah said. "They're pissant racketeers, shakin' down Medicare and Medicaid."

"A racket, you say. To cheat the government. You learned all this . . . in how many days? Three? Four?"

Maytubby stood shoulder to shoulder with Bond. More like shoulder to elbow. "Dan—Agent Scrooby—Hannah is right. Your time is precious, so I'll ask you to record this on your cell audio. I'm going at the quick march."

Scrooby exhaled loudly and rolled his eyes. "Quick march." He reached in his pants pocket and pulled out his phone. He laid it on the table and fingered its screen. When he withdrew his hand, Maytubby began.

"Doug Verner's body was discovered in Pennington Creek by a deaf Chickasaw boy, Jason Laber, who lives with this mother on the property. The body was outfitted with fly-fishing gear recently purchased by Dr. Patton Archerd. Dr. Archerd is a podiatrist practicing in Highland Park, Texas. He is also a member of the Chickasaw Nation."

Scrooby said, "Wait. A Chickasaw foot doctor in Highland Park? One of the richest cities in Texas?"

Chief Fox said, "Why should that surprise you, Dan? We have an astronaut from the Nation. The US congressman from this district is a Chickasaw."

Scrooby spread his left hand and wagged it at Fox. "Okay, okay. Got it."

"Hannah and I—on our own time—drove to Dr. Archerd's clinic in Highland Park. It's called Foot Kingdom. We were, uh, undercover."

"Wearing crap stuff," Bond said.

"Four minutes," Scrooby said.

"Security took us to a fake groundskeeping building, where we were asked to fill out patient forms. One of our proctors, now the prisoner Smoot"—Maytubby cocked his head toward the jail—"is likely Doug

Verner's killer. The length of rebar you want is being kept by a liquor store owner in Coalgate. The rebar near Verner's car was a plant."

Scrooby grimaced. "Coalgate. What—"

"It's his time," Hannah barked.

Maytubby said, "Hannah watched the Verner house and saw two new vehicles with Texas dealer plates. Her big Steiner binoculars came in handy. She and I traced these plates to the Sitka Auto Ranch in Plano. Coming back from Dallas, we found the sporting goods store where Archerd bought his duds and tackle. At the Auto Ranch, we saw prisoner Nail"—again Maytubby cocked his head toward the cells—"in the seat of a medical transport van with a Gautier Transportation sign." He spelled the name for the recorder. "We tailed him to a post office and an abandoned house and back to Plano. He was likely gauging mileage for false claims."

Bond said, "The forms Bill and me filled out for Smoot at the foot doc's place had post office boxes in Sherman already filled in for our addresses."

Scrooby now looked down at the table, his eyes coming to life. He didn't mention the countdown.

"Sunday night, I called around," Maytubby said, "and found Verner's smashed car on Mill Creek. Agent Cable investigated that."

Hannah exhaled through her nose.

"Then I drove past the Verner house and saw there was a convention. I parked far away and ran to the house from the east. From the carport, I heard Bradley the lawyer, Jimmy Nail, a guy I can't identify, and Smoot—Smoot a little later—talking shop. That's when I learned about Nail trashing Curt Fenton's car, and the unnamed guy calling Curt in Texas to snitch on his wife and Verner. Also about the rebar plant. Before they heard me and chased me off—a stranger, as far as they knew—I searched the bed of Nail's pickup, which belongs to Eliphaz Valentine." Maytubby looked at Fox, who nodded. "Also known as Tiny. I also searched the bed of Smoot's 1957 Chevy short bed." Maytubby reached in his pants pocket and pulled out three evidence bags, which he tossed on the table. "I didn't gather them on the Verner property. Ten minutes ago, I inventoried both trucks in impound and retrieved the evidence there."

A few seconds passed while Scrooby, Fox, and Magaw looked at the bags.

"I found Nail and Tiny in their lair outside Bromide on a hunch," Maytubby said.

"Lare?" Scrooby said.

"Hideout," Maytubby said.

"'*Hunch*'?" Hannah protested. "Sergeant Maytubby hid his—"

Maytubby waved her off and shook his head. Hannah scowled and stepped back.

He pointed to the bags. "That Woolly Bugger, I found in Smoot's truck bed when the gang was at the Verners' house. I learned at the tackle store that Patton Archerd bought one—along with the rod and probably the rest—shortly before the murder. The butts in the paper bag are for Tiny's and Nail's DNA. The fake ruby, I found in the bed of Tiny's truck. Wait on that."

Bond cleared her throat. "We got to back up. The deaf boy, Jason? He trapped coons at night down on Pennington. Bill got a sign-language expert from the Chickasaws to ask him what he saw the night before he found the body. You go on, Bill."

Maytubby took the transcript from his pocket and laid it on the table. "Jason was trapping late at night when he saw a tall man—in the light of the man's flashlight—pulling a cart away from Pennington Creek. He said the man was wearing on his head something like a rooster's comb. He also said the cart had shiny things like diamonds on it.

"I believe that man was Eliphaz Valentine. Known as Tiny. Also in lockup. Dollars to duck shot, he lugged Verner's body to the creek in that cart. More about the cart in a minute. He saw Jason and set someone on him and his mother. The mother, Deborah Laber, called me the next morning at three a.m. and said she heard a truck on Bellwood Road near her house. When I arrived, this man was trying to kick in her door. I knocked him down, but he escaped. I photographed his sneaker print using my own sneakers for scale."

Bond rested her hands on her duty belt. "Bill brought Jason and his mom to my house later in the morning so I could look after 'em. The boy brought his four-ten, which came in handy later that night. Smoot and Possum Face—"

"The lawyer Bradley," Maytubby said.

"Him," Bond said. "They found my house and came after us. I called Bill. They were plannin' to kill all of us in the house and burn it down. Me and Jason kept the maggots busy until Bill and this guy that Tiny sued for land—LeeRoy Sickles—showed up and run 'em to ground."

Scrooby had ceased blowing. He stared at Bond and Maytubby with the wide eyes of a child being read to.

"Before I got to Hannah's house . . ." Maytubby looked at his watch. "Oh, sorry. I'm out of time." He and Bond stood silent and looked at the overhead lights.

Scrooby recovered. He scowled. And blew. "Go. On," he said to the table.

"Before I got to Hannah's house, I drove to Tiny and Nail's hideout south of Bromide. They caught me, and Jimmy knocked me cold. When I came to, I was under the homemade chariot Jason had seen on Pennington. Fake jewels and all. Part of his Roman soldier playacting for the Holy City of Jerusalem he was building of rock he quarried on Butcher Pen Road. While he was on the SSI dole. That's what brought him into the ring. I think Nail discovered a fellow grifter. I believe you'll find a Trojans or Spartans marching band helmet Tiny used as part of his Roman getup. And that red bristle in Jason's trap I left in the evidence bag at Pennington? I think that helmet fell into the trap and that red bristle comes from the helmet's crest. The guy Hannah mentioned—LeeRoy Sickles—saved my bacon with his double-barrel ten-gauge.

"After Sickles and I were done at Hannah's place . . ." Maytubby turned to Deputy Bond.

"Bill and me drove back to Bromide and waited for Tiny and Jimmy Nail to get back to their truck, which LeeRoy had drove Bill away in, almost to Bromide Road. LeeRoy had let the air out of one of their front tires after the excape. Bill and me cuffed 'em and hauled 'em in."

Maytubby nodded once. "End of story," he said.

"Except . . ." Hannah unsnapped a compartment on her duty belt and pulled out a plastic bag containing a scrap of paper. She laid the bag on the table. "I found this gas receipt in the Blue River Fishing Area, just off Highway Seven." She looked at the sheriff. "On my lunch hour." Then she turned back to Scrooby. "It's from a Quik Trip in Plano, dated Thursday. My guess is the foot doctor. The cameras at the store might show someone else in the vehicle."

As Bond and Maytubby walked from the table back to the west wall of the room, there was much throat-clearing among the other lawmen. Scrooby reached for his phone, then withdrew his hand.

There was an acre of silence.

Scrooby blew and then closed his eyes and pinched his nose. "Okay," he said to the floor in front of Maytubby and Bond. "If any of this is true, what's your best guess about how the foot doctor—"

"Patton Archerd," Maytubby said.

"Yeah. How'd he figure in the murder?"

"We don't know," Maytubby said. "That's going to be up to you and the Civil Medicaid Fraud Division of the Texas Attorney General's Office. Archerd instigated the fraud ring, almost certainly. We also know from a clerk in the tackle shop that he took a very recent interest in trout fishing in the Blue. Just before the last day of the season. That looks bad. But my hunch is that Smoot set Archerd up somehow and swiped his gear to put on Verner's body. That way, Archerd wouldn't be a suspect."

"Stupid," Scrooby said.

"Fealty," Maytubby said.

"What?"

"Loyalty to his master," Maytubby said.

Scrooby shook his head and scowled. "And again, where, exactly, is the rebar Smoot supposedly used to kill Verner?"

Maytubby pulled a pen from his pocket and, on Scrooby's Styrofoam box, wrote Lorenza Mercante's name and the address of her liquor store in Coalgate. "Smoot and Gautier Transportation were using the late Wiley Bates's shack."

"The incinerated guy. How'd you get down there so fast?" Scrooby said.

"I flew that old Cessna I used to follow the hired assassin Hillers two years ago. On the way to Coalgate, I saw where Tiny dragged one of LeeRoy Sickles's old cars out of a junk heap. I think you'll find it was the beltless 1956 Hudson someone towed to Honey Wash to, uh, throw us off the scent."

Scrooby gargled his contempt. Then he made the "OK" finger circle and held it to his forehead. Cyclops, for dumb crackers.

Now Scrooby touched his phone and stuffed it in his pocket. He looked at Maytubby. "How did you learn to fly?"

Maytubby said, "When I was in college at St. John's in Santa Fe, there was an older student in my class. Rich family in Vermont. Before he came to college, he got certified as a flight instructor. And a multiengine pilot. He was having trouble in ancient Greek and asked me to tutor him. In exchange, he taught me to fly and paid for the plane rental." All eyes were on him.

Scrooby said, "Ancient Greek. Huh." He shook his head.

Hannah rolled her eyes.

Scrooby planted his hands on the table and rose. He looked around the room. "Gentlemen," he said. "And Deputy Bond." He nodded to each and tossed his breakfast box in a trash can. "Sheriff Magaw, I'd like a word with you. Alone."

Fox, Maytubby, and Bond filed out of the room.

CHAPTER 31

Three weeks later, on a Saturday morning in late April, Maytubby, Jill, Hannah, Maxine Fenton, Deb Laber, and LeeRoy Sickles sat around two shoved-together tables at the Aldridge Hotel Coffee Shop in Ada. On a wall-mounted television, an Oklahoma City meteorologist warned of a tornado outbreak in the afternoon.

Sickles sat to Hannah's right. He wore denim overalls and a white dress shirt with an ancient black tie that disappeared under the denim bib. His arms danced on the table, cufflinks clacking. Hannah was in uniform for an afternoon shift in Tish. A waitress brought waters and handed around plastic menus.

Maxine sat on Hannah's left. She was thinner and had dark moons under her eyes.

The table was quiet while everyone looked at their menus.

Hannah slapped hers down first. LeeRoy followed suit. One by one, the menus hit the table. The waitress came with coffee for all.

Hannah, Sickles, and Deb Laber ordered breakfast specials with eggs, bacon, hash browns, and biscuits and gravy. Maytubby, Jill, and Maxine Fenton ordered oatmeal with raisins.

Hannah said, "You didn't invite Agent Scrooby, Bill? He loves him some biscuits and scalded crow."

Sickles said, "Scalded crow. Hee hee hee. Good one, Big Sister." His head bobbed, and he reached for the cigarette pack in the top pocket of his overalls. Then he stopped, adjusted his black plastic glasses, and stuck out his chin.

Hannah gave him the side eye but half smiled.

Maytubby said, "I did. He sends his regrets."

"I bet," Hannah said.

Maytubby said, "Introductions." He leaned against Jill. "This is Jill Milton. I am her fiancé. She's a nutritionist with the Chickasaw Nation." All nodded in her direction. He extended a palm toward Deb. "This is Deb Laber." She nodded. "Her son Jason helped us crack the case."

Deb Laber interrupted him. "Sergeant Maytubby came in the dead of night to drive off a man trying to kick in our door. And Deputy Bond kept Jason and me safe in her house until the worst was over."

Sickles said, "Didn't hurt that your deaf boy had a shotgun."

Hannah touched his shoulder and shook her head.

"Well, it didn't, did it? Hee hee hee."

"Hannah?" Maytubby said.

Bond laid her hand on Maxine Fenton's shoulder. "This here is Maxine Fenton. Her husband was framed for the murder of Doug Verner."

Maxine Fenton nodded solemnly. "Thank you for inviting me," she said. Jill put her left arm around her. Fenton began to sob and said, "Curt is back on the road. I do want to learn what happened after he was freed from jail."

Hannah frowned deeply and shook her head. After a beat, she pointed at LeeRoy and said, "This Gomer is LeeRoy Sickles. He spied on two of the crooks and saved Bill's life out by Bromide. Then he run the killer Smoot down outside my house." She turned to Maytubby. "Steel-Toe *was* the killer, right?"

Maytubby said, "OSBI matched DNA on the rebar he tossed out of his pickup in Coalgate to both Smoot and . . . I'm sorry, Ms. Fenton . . ."

Maxine Fenton nodded and grasped Jill's arm.

". . . Doug Verner. Smoot has been charged with first-degree murder."

"All the skinny, Bill," Hannah said. "We're gonna eat in a minute."

Maytubby took a sip of water and set his plastic tumbler down. "Texas Medicaid Fraud was already investigating Patton Archerd when Hannah and I horned in. They used what we found to close in on Gautier Transportation, the Sitka Auto Ranch in Plano, and Ella Bednar. The Oklahoma Medicaid Fraud Control Unit is partnering with Texas and OSBI to target Valentine, Nail, Smoot, Tula Verner, and the lawyer Bradley. More importantly, all these people have been charged with conspiracy to commit murder."

"Good," Maxine Fenton croaked.

Maytubby drank more water. "Deb, the state police have impounded the homemade chariot Tiny Valentine made, and . . ." He frowned and shook his head as he looked at Maxine Fenton. "Again, sorry, Maxine."

Maxine nodded as tears ran down her cheeks. She stuck up her right thumb in approval.

"Doug Verner's DNA was found in the bed of the chariot. Tiny carted his body to the creek in it."

Deb said, "The diamonds Jason saw on the cart."

"Yes," Maytubby said. "And in the chariot, they also found a plastic Roman centurion marching-band helmet with a red crest."

"The rooster comb," Deb said.

Hannah said, "Your boy paid close attention."

LeeRoy's cufflinks skated on the table before he clapped his left hand over his mouth and shook his head.

"He always has," Deb Laber said.

Maytubby said, "There was one more fellow with the gang at Tula's house the night I eavesdropped. I never did catch his name. Scrooby told me that Tiny has cooperated with the investigation."

"To keep his sorry butt out of Leavenworth," Hannah said.

LeeRoy was convulsed with glee but said nothing.

"His name is Gautier. He started the fake medical transit company that bears his name. Also charged in the murder conspiracy."

Hannah said, "What about the boozer who tag-teamed with Steel-Toe at the groundskeeping place to sign you and me up, Bill?"

"Archerd's brother-in-law. Died of a heart attack two weeks ago."

Hannah nodded and drank some coffee.

"And Eph?" Maytubby asked Hannah.

She waved her hand in the air. "Eph's Eph. His face looks like a barnyard, though."

The waitress served everyone and refilled all the coffees. The table's sounds—snapping cutlery and slushing ice in water glasses—joined those of the dining room. The absence of voices also marked the aftermath with Southern Plains stoicism.

It also reminded Maytubby of a line from his favorite poet, Emily Dickinson—a New Englander. "After great pain, a formal feeling comes." The friends at the table did indeed eat formally. Even LeeRoy Sickles, whose hands moved steadily. Even Hannah, who took small bites. Jill kept her arm around Maxine's shoulders.

* * *

After the waitress cleared the plates and handed Maytubby the check, everyone rose. Deb Laber nodded to Hannah, who nodded back. Deb walked toward the door.

Jill hugged Maxine Fenton. Maxine turned to Hannah, looked up into her face, and said, "You understood Curt and me from the first minute you walked into our house."

Hannah frowned and nodded. "Okay," she said, holding out her hand. They shook, and Maxine walked away.

LeeRoy sidled up to Hannah. She looked down at him. He slid his thumbs under the straps of his overalls. "Hey, Tall Drink," he said. "Now that Tiny's put away and you got no more papers to serve me." His head bobbed, but his body stilled. "Come see me sometime. We can shoot off my back porch. If you drank, I got some Old Crow left over from my partyin' days."

Hannah glanced at Maytubby and then back at Sickles. "I might just do," she said. Sickles giggled and danced out the restaurant door.

Hannah faced Maytubby and Jill Milton. "Oh, Lord," she said, and then followed LeeRoy out the door.

Maytubby paid the bill. He put his arm around Jill's waist. They stopped and looked at the framed lobby card for *Tulsa*. "Feeling tempestuous?" she said.

He bent his head to her neck and whispered, "You know Quaker Oats drive me wild."

ACKNOWLEDGMENTS

As always, profound thanks to my gifted editor Michael Carr, who gets the Southern Plains.

I am deeply grateful to my dear friends Sarah Miracle and Jill Fox, who advise me on matters of tribal health education.

Jason Eyechabbe patiently taught me the little Chickasaw I know, and also demonstrated the fundamentals of stickball. Jason O'Neill, former Chickasaw Lighthorse Chief of Police, patiently explained the basics of tribal jurisdiction. Any errors on this score are mine alone. Staff at the Lighthorse Police have answered my telephone queries in helpful detail.

Warm thanks to friends who have answered queries along the way: Karleene Smith, Joel Morgan, Peter Chase, Francesca Novello, Dale Wares, Rick Poland, Chris Suit, Desiree Hupy, and Michael Hahn.

I am indebted to three American Sign Language experts—Nikki Boehme, Matt Dickens, and Alicia Martin—for helping me revise scenes with Jason Laber. Any stumbles are down to me.

Robert Kelson and Paul Swenson, retired law enforcement officers, and Jerry Carter, forensic firearms examiner at the Oklahoma State Bureau of Investigation, answered many questions about police procedure. I take responsibility for any mistakes on this score.

Abrazos to Jenny Vigil, owner of Norman's Gray Owl Coffee, and to my brilliant barista friends there and at Michelangelo's: Laura, Andrew, Chris, Braden, Roshni, Erika, Emily, Katie, Caleb, Lucas, Anastasia, Gavin, and Sierra.

A salute to book designers Zena Coffman and Djamika Smith and to the audio voice of the series, Mark Bramhall. Hearty thanks to Danuta Press, who presided elegantly over the Norman rollout of *Greasy Bend*, and to Greg Boguslawski, Blackstone's road wizard.

Stout thanks to my witty and generous agent, Richard Curtis.

Hearty praise for Blackstone's ace publicist Lauren Maturo, who labors tirelessly to promote her writers' work and raise their spirits. She herself is a fine writer.

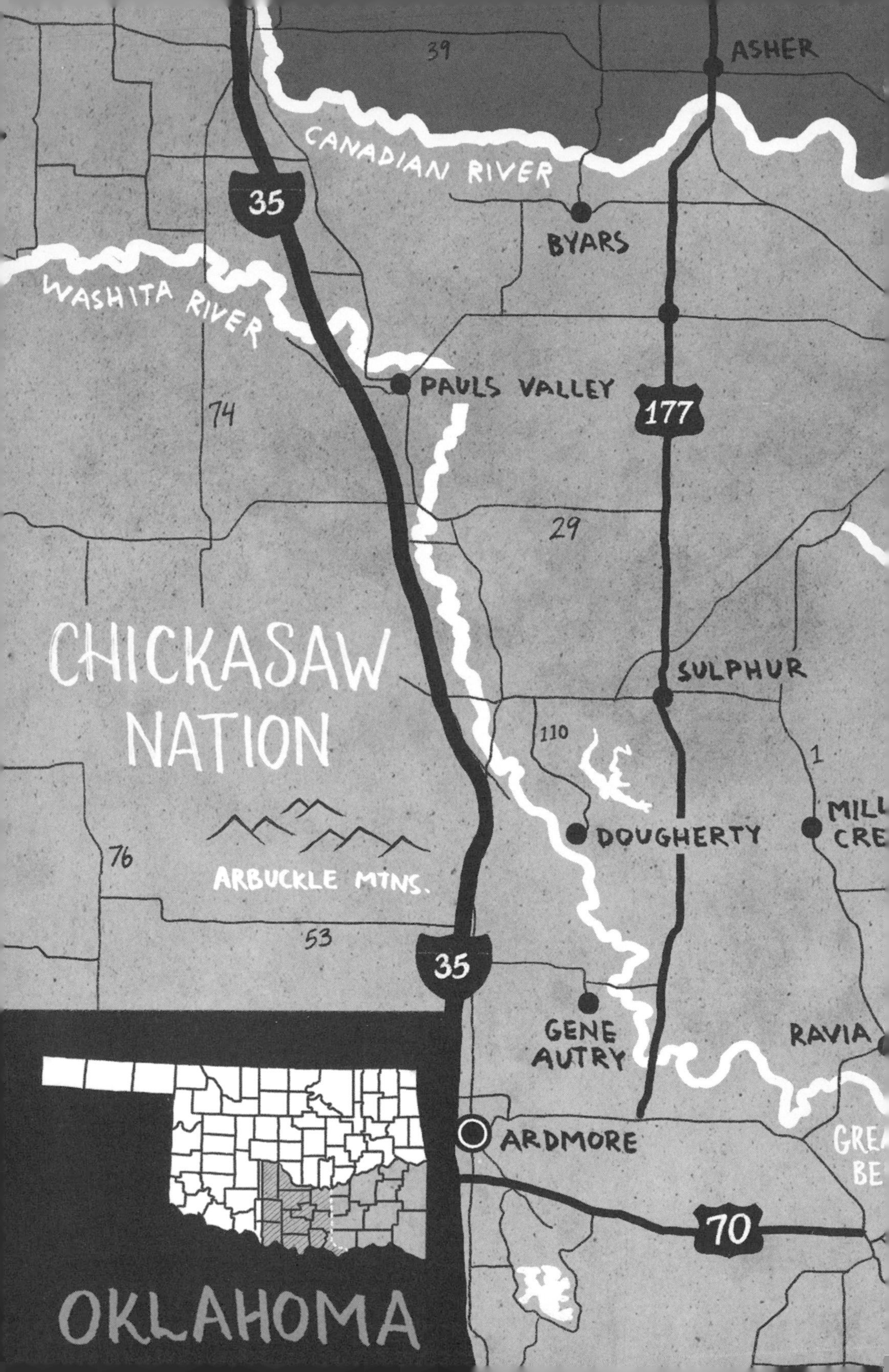

39
ASHER
CANADIAN RIVER
35
BYARS
WASHITA RIVER
PAULS VALLEY
177
74
29
CHICKASAW NATION
SULPHUR
110
1
DOUGHERTY
MILL CRE
76
ARBUCKLE MTNS.
53
35
GENE AUTRY
RAVIA
ARDMORE
GREA BE
70
OKLAHOMA